The Undetective

BRUCE GRAEME

 Moonstone Press

This edition published in 2020 by Moonstone Press
www.moonstonepress.co.uk

Introduction © 2020 Moonstone Press

Originally published in 1962 by Hutchinson & Co Ltd
The Undetective © 1962 the Estate of Graham Montague Jeffries,
writing as Bruce Graeme

ISBN 978-1-899000-24-1
eISBN 978-1-899000-25-8

A CIP catalogue record for this book is available from the British Library

Text designed and typeset by Tetragon, London
Cover illustration by Jason Anscomb
Printed and bound by CPI Group (UK) Ltd, Croydon, CR0 4YY

Contents

Introduction

In *The Undetective*, a mystery writer finds himself drawn into a real-world murder, to dramatic and sometimes comical effect. This was a recurring theme of the work of Bruce Graeme—dozens of his books feature mystery writers, novelists or movie script writers as the protagonists and melded crime fiction and real crime in an entertaining way. Graeme was a pseudonym of Graham Montague Jeffries (1900–82), a prolific writer of more than one hundred crime and adventure stories over a sixty-plus year career. Born 23 May 1900, Jeffries grew up in London, served in the Queen's Westminster Rifles Regiment during the First World War, worked as a reporter in the 1920s for the *Middlesex County Times*, and was a film producer during the 1940s. After marrying Lorna Helene Louch in 1925, the couple resided with their two children, Roderic and Guillaine, in an Elizabethan farmhouse in East Ashford, Kent.

Jeffries also wrote under the pseudonyms David Graeme (claiming he was Bruce's cousin), Peter Bourne, Jeffrey Montague, Fielding Hope and Roderic Hastings. Aside from stand-alone novels like *The Undetective*, Jeffries created six series characters: bookseller Theodore Terhune, Superintendent William Stevens, Inspector Allain of the Sûreté, Detective Sergeant Robert Mather, Inspector Auguste Jantry, and—the character Jeffries is probably best known for—Richard Verrell, alias Blackshirt, a professional thief who becomes a successful crime novelist.

Blackshirt and later his son Anthony Verrell (aka Lord Blackshirt) appeared in over thirty books between 1926 and 1969. Jeffries published the initial Blackshirt stories between 1929 and 1949, and his son Roderic wrote an additional twenty novels for the series starting in 1952 under the name Roderic Graeme. Eventually, Roderic Jeffries began writing crime and suspense fiction under his own name, as well as under two other pen names, like his pseudonym-loving father.

In *The Undetective*, mystery writer Iain Carter develops a nom de plume for a new series of police procedurals based on a bit of 'insider' knowledge. His purpose is achieved beyond his wildest dreams, but soon the situation spins out of control as the tax authorities, the press, and the police themselves become very interested in the real identity of 'John Ky. Lowell'. The plot complications thicken when a murder occurs and the pseudonymous crime writer becomes a prime suspect.

The book within the book, *The Undetective*—the fictional John Ky. Lowell's first successful outing—is a police procedural, albeit a satirical one, and it's enjoyable to see a tongue-in-cheek, Sixties-style take on the genre. The first police procedural (where the methodology of detection is based on real-life police work) is often cited as *V as in Victim* by Lawrence Treat (1945), but for many readers it was Hillary Waugh's *Last Seen Wearing* (1952) that launched the genre. John Creasey's 'Gideon' books were the most successful British police novels of the period; starting with *Gideon's Day* (1955) and running through twenty-one books to *Gideon's Drive* (1976), published three years after his death. Another astonishingly prolific writer, Creasey published more than five hundred novels under twenty-eight different pseudonyms during his forty-one-year career. One reason for the pseudonyms was that booksellers complained that he dominated the "C" section in bookshops. In his spare time, the energetic Creasey founded the Crime Writers' Association in 1953, and Jeffries succeeded him as chairman in 1956.

A fun bonus to *The Undetective* is in the copious references to the CWA, which mix fiction and reality. Contemporary members are mentioned, such as Michael Gilbert, Ernest Dudley and Margot Bennett, and one scene takes place at a CWA meeting. There is even a satirical dig at British crime critic Julian Symons, who reviews unkindly one of the books Iain continues to publish under his own name. One wonders if in real life Graeme (or one of Jeffries' other aliases) had been subjected to a pungent review by Mr. Symons.

Jeffries and Creasey had plentiful company in their use of pseudonyms in the crime-writing genre. A comprehensive list of pen names would be an impossible task, but a quick tally from Barzun & Taylor's *A Catalogue of Crime* (1971) reveals over ninety authors who wrote under a different name. Some authors used pen names to protect their more literary publications (J. I. M. Stewart writing as Michael Innes), some women adopted male pen names (Lucy Beatrice Malleson writing as Anthony Gilbert), some chose deliberately androgynous monikers to avoid gender stereotyping (Eric Stanley Gardner as A. A. Fair). And some, like Creasey and Jeffries, were simply so prolific that publishers felt the market would be unable to cope with their level of output.

The 1950s and early 1960s witnessed a 'decline of deference' in Britain that emerged from the gradual breakdown of post-war social consensus, but the legitimacy of the police remained intact throughout the period. In fact, after the interwar years where the British bobby was a long-established figure of fun to be mocked by eccentric amateur detectives, the iconic film representation of the 1950s was PC George Dixon, featuring in *The Blue Lamp* (1950) and later in the BBC television series *Dixon of Dock Green*, which ran for an astonishing twenty-one years from 1955 to 1976 (an interesting parallel to Creasey's career). Dixon was the reassuring manifestation of calm rational authority that would continue to dominate cinema screens until the early 1960s. One wonders if the chance to poke fun at this staid image of the constabulary was an additional incentive to an author who liked to experiment. It is a tribute to Jeffries' willing to try new forms that *The Undetective* emerges as one part police procedural, one part satire of the publishing industry, and one part traditional murder mystery.

Though he sold over four million books during his career, Jeffries has been unjustly neglected as one of the most original crime fiction writers of his period. Moonstone Press is delighted to introduce *The Undetective* to a new generation of readers.

I t was my own fault, of course. I realized that when it was too late. But this I say with absolute sincerity: if I could have foreseen the consequences I should have hesitated a long time before making fools of the police, before exasperating them to the point when they welcomed an opportunity which was not only in the line of duty, but, simultaneously, gave them what they hoped would be a chance of getting their own back on me.

Here is my biography, previous to my meeting Susan for the first time.

CARTER, Iain Wallace, Author and Barrister-at-Law, eldest son of Robert Iain Carter, solicitor, of Two Cedars, Cornwall Road, and Jane Margaret Wallace. *Age:* 25 years, four months. *Educated:* West London Preparatory School: Arundel. *Details of career:* Admitted Gray's Inn, published Barrister-at-Law, served one year's pupillage in Chambers of Gordon Macintosh, with signal lack of success, retired gracefully from the Law to take up Literature. Cajolled, pestered, and practically blackmailed publisher-uncle, James Dougall of Dougall and Smith, to publish first novel. Miraculously, it nearly did not lose money, on the strength of which Dougall and Smith published the next five books.

I'll say this for my parents, my father in particular. They were sports. In spite of their bitter disappointment that I was hopeless as a lawyer, they did not rail at me as they might have done. As Father said: 'To have as near relative a solicitor, who could pass on as many briefs as he could handle, is a gift of God for which a newly called barrister would normally give five years of his life; but it's your life, Iain, and I do not intend to try and influence you in the way you lead it.'

'You wouldn't have briefed me for long. You'd have lost all your clients.'

He sighed. 'I must admit that you were peculiarly inept. Perhaps you have made a wise decision. What do you propose to do instead?'

'Write.'

'Write!' He looked startled.

'Books. Detective stories.'

'Good gracious! But what do you know about writing books?'

'Nothing, so far. But don't forget writing is in the family. There's Cousin Philip, Uncle William, and great-great-Grandfather Septimus. To say nothing of Uncle James, who is a publisher.'

'True, true. Though I have not heard that any of them made a fortune from their books,' he drily added.

'I know, that's why I shall have to take a job.'

'What as?'

'I haven't thought that much ahead, but as long as it brings me in enough to live for a few years, until I get established…'

'You do not have to take a position, Iain. I am not a wealthy man by some standards, but neither am I poor. I will give you an allowance of six hundred a year for some years—'

'No, Father, I won't take it…'

But ultimately I did, and ultimately I wrote my first novel, which Uncle James offered to publish on normal first-novel terms. £100 advance on account of royalties of 10 per cent to 2,500 copies, 12½ per cent from 2,500 to 5,000 copies, and 15 per cent thereafter.

'Accepted,' I promptly agreed.

He appeared not to hear me but continued: 'Dougall and Smith to handle all subsidiary rights—'

'What!'

'Fifty per cent to you for paper-back rights, eighty-five per cent on sales to the U.S.A. and foreign translations, eighty-five per cent—'

'No.'

He paused, looked up. 'No what?'

'I'm not giving you any cut in subsidiary rights.'

'In that case—'

'I have been told of at least six publishing firms who do not ask for subsidiary rights.'

'In that case, naturally, you will offer your book to them.'

'But you are my uncle,' I protested. 'Let's keep it in the family.'

'I am also a business man, not a philanthropist. In these days of high production costs a publisher considers himself lucky not to lose money publishing fiction. It is only by having a share in the sale of subsidiary rights that he can hope to make profits.'

'If you are *not* a philanthropist why are you offering to publish my book?'

As a Scot, Uncle James isn't so easily defeated in argument. 'Merely because you are my nephew,' he blandly replied. 'It is your idea to keep it in the family.'

So *One Case for O'Shea* was published. Thanks to its being adapted as a radio play for B.B.C.'s *Saturday Night Theatre*, it nearly did not lose money, as recorded in my biography. As ninety-nine out of every hundred detective stories aren't heard in *Saturday Night Theatre*, or on any other night in the week, it is amazing how publishers continue to operate. Perhaps Mr. Parkinson will consider the problem and one day propound another of his famous Laws.

Father and Mother were very pleased with *One Case for O'Shea*. 'Could be worse,' Father admitted after he had read it. 'Blood tells,' he added. I knew he was thinking of great-great-Grandfather Septimus.

'Pity your knowledge of the law isn't as sound as your writing,' he added in that dry way of his. 'But, then, you are only a barrister.'

Even Anne was so proud of being connected with me that for at least one week she carried the book about with her wherever she went—Anne's my kid sister, four years younger than I.

So much for those earlier years. On the eve of publication of my sixth book, *Shadow Crime*, Father gave a party for the two of us: it chanced to be his fifty-second birthday. That night the house was burgled. Whether it was a case of cause and effect I cannot say. Perhaps the line of parked cars outside the house attracted the attention of a passing burglar.

The following morning a detective from our division called on Father. 'Detective-Constable Meredith,' he introduced himself in a crisp voice.

The two men shook hands. 'My son, Iain.'

'Mr. Iain Carter! The writer of detective stories?'

'Fame at last! What do you think of that, Father? I'm beginning to be known by name.'

Meredith grinned. 'I'm a prolific reader of detective stories, sir. There are not many published I don't read.'

I wasn't going to be robbed of my first sweet moment of success. 'You recognized my name, that's something.'

'It's part of our training to remember names and faces. But I like your books better than most, if you don't mind me saying so.'

'Mind! I'm overjoyed.'

Father coughed.

Meredith looked embarrassed. 'I'm sorry, sir.'

Father chuckled. 'You don't have to be, but I have an appointment at the office in...' He glanced at his watch. 'Half an hour's time.'

'I won't keep you long, sir, just long enough for a list of the stolen property...'

Father gave this, and left for his appointment. Meredith questioned me for a time, but there was not much I could tell him. In any case, I had a feeling that he had already guessed the identity of the burglar. When I bluntly put this question to him he laughed.

'I should have remembered that you have some knowledge of crime and police investigation. Your guess is a good one. Everything about this job bears the hallmark of an old friend of mine who's been inside seven or eight times.'

'They don't learn, do they? Might as well leave a visiting card, some of them. What will you do? Ask him to prove an alibi?'

'Yes, and quickly, before he has time to cook one up. I may be lucky and find him still in bed.'

Meredith not only found the man in bed, but some of the stolen goods still underneath it. I met him again at the subsequent magistrates' court proceedings. After the thief had wisely pleaded 'Guilty', and the case had been sent for sentence at the next Assizes, I asked the constable whether he would care to have a drink with me at the *George and Dragon*.

He looked at his watch, and nodded. 'I think I can spare a few minutes, sir, thanks to Tom pleading guilty.'

We chattered awhile over our beers. I found myself beginning to like the man. I judged him to be not much older than I. With plenty of blue-black hair, brown eyes, quick speech, uninhibited laughter, and a slightly exotic cast of features he gave me the impression of being partly European. Italian, perhaps. His figure was slight, athletic. I wasn't surprised to hear him mention squash-racquets.

'Do you play much?' I asked him.

'As often as I can.' He grinned. 'Not as often as I would like to.'

'Are you good?'

'So-so, not match-winning standard.'

'Care to give me a game some time? I need some hard exercise.'

'Love to,' he promptly answered. Then he looked at me with those bright, speculative eyes of his. 'How good are *you*?'

'So-so, not match-winning standard.'

'Fair enough.' He laughed, and the genuine carefree note in it made me think that he was glad to have an opportunity of laughing with someone unconnected with his work.

Later that week we played squash, and each found that the other had told the truth about his play. We were both reasonably good; a fair match for the other. We had a thoroughly energetic and enjoyable half-hour's play, and had no difficulty at all in subsequently downing a pint of bitter apiece.

That was the first of several meetings at the squash-courts; irregular, by nature of Meredith's work. A detective's time is never his own, I learned. For instance, one night, as he was leaving his office to keep an appointment with me, the Super met him face to face.

'Where are you off to?' the Super grimly asked. 'Squash again?' He didn't have to be a detective to deduce this from the sports-bag which Meredith was carrying.

'Yes, sir.'

'That's what you think. There's a juicy one just reported from three, Thurlow Road. There's only you and me available.'

'Have I time to 'phone, sir?'

'No. Tell the desk-sergeant. He will give the good news to your friend.'

So that night I was deprived of a game. It was no particular consolation for me to read, the next morning, gory reports of the 'juicy one' which had been responsible: a couple of women brutally murdered by a sex-maniac.

It so happened that this particular crime was to have indirect consequences for me. The next time Meredith turned up for a game of squash he was accompanied by a girl.

'Sorry to inflict this upon you, Iain,' he apologized. 'Susan, meet Iain Carter. Iain, this is my sister, Mrs. Poynter. Don't blame me for bringing her. It wasn't my idea.'

'It was mine, Mr. Carter. You see, I have tickets for the theatre tonight and asked Edward to take me in place of my escort, who had to call off in order to fly to New York on behalf of his firm. Edward generously said he would, but when he mentioned something about 'phoning you to postpone the game I wouldn't let him. I know what happened the last time you were supposed to play.'

I cursed my luck. Why did she have to be Mrs. Somebody? She really was a honey.

'Please don't apologize, Mrs. Poynter. We can fix another evening—'

'Nonsense, you are going to play right now, and I am going to watch you.'

'But the theatre?'

'There will still be time if you don't take too long over your drinks afterwards, which Edward tells me are a "must". I shall watch you from the gallery.'

I glanced questioningly at Meredith, who grinned back. 'It's no use arguing with Susan. You always lose. Let's get changed.'

We changed and stepped into the court. As I closed the door behind me and glanced up at the gallery I was unexpectedly filled with an overwhelming desire to win, to beat Meredith with a decisive score. I slammed a practice ball against the service wall, and full-volleyed as it shot back at me. A pretty shot, quite something to see. And again. I warmed with jubilation. My eye was in.

I played harder than I had ever played before. I won the first game fairly easily, but, after a speculative glance first at me and then at the gallery, Meredith began to put on the pressure.

Long rallies followed. I'll swear we both played like champions. Up—down, left—right, this corner—that corner... It was a game in a thousand, but I won it by the odd point.

'Bloody swank!' he whispered as we crossed sides, but his grin was full of mischief and good-humour. I knew he had guessed what I was doing, and didn't mind. Indeed, I realize now that he was deliberately playing right up to his best, to force me to do the same and so make my victory all the more convincing. Which it was. She began to clap our more spectacular rallies and our clever, crafty placing.

I won again, and again; though not by the decisive score I had originally conceived. But this I no longer minded, for two reasons. In themselves, the games were too wonderful for me to care who won. Secondly, I knew I had achieved my objective. As an exhibitionist I was pretty good.

As we re-entered the dressing-room to strip for a shower, Meredith clapped me on the shoulder. 'Next time you bring *your* sister,' he suggested.

We had drinks at the *Royal*. Meredith had nearly finished his when he slapped the tankard down on the bar with a thump.

'I've had me an idea, Susan. What about your taking Iain instead of me?'

'No—' I protested.

She didn't give me a chance to finish. 'A perfectly lovely idea— that is, if you are free, Mr. Carter. I know Edward is tired and would much rather go to bed. With a brother's frankness he told me so earlier on. I should not have asked him if I had known anyone nicer to accompany me at the last moment.'

'But... but...' I didn't know how to continue. 'Your husband— will he mind?' I stammered.

Meredith fondly slipped an arm about his sister's shoulders. 'Susan is a widow,' he said sombrely.

Those four words made my evening.

The more I saw of Susan, the more I felt attracted towards her; not so much for her natural loveliness, although in itself this was enough to make any man become her victim, as for an intangible quality, a charm, which made her the nicest person I had met.

One evening, while Meredith and I waited for a free court, I asked him: 'How long has your sister been a widow?'

'Something over two years. About two and a half, I'd say.'

'She must have married young.'

'She did. Too young.'

I sensed by the way he spoke that he had disapproved of the marriage. 'What happened to him?'

'Car accident. Burnt to a cinder. He was on his way back from Toronto to Montreal when he hit the back of an articulated trunk, skidded, hit a wall, and overturned. Before the truck-driver could pull him out, the car exploded into flames. That was that.'

'Speeding?'

'Like crazy, according to evidence. Ruddy fool. Friends said he had twice been warned he'd get his if he didn't watch out. Thank God Susan wasn't with him.'

Amen to that!

'Were they holidaying in Canada?'

'He was living there. Susan was on holiday, staying with an aunt, when she first met him. He had emigrated there ten years previously. Had a job in an accountant's office. Susan fell for him hook, line, and sinker. They were married within three weeks.' He laughed shortly. 'Funny, isn't it; none of us ever met him. We couldn't afford to go out for the wedding, and he was killed, fourteen months after marriage, before they could return to England even for a holiday—or a vacation, as Susan has learned to say. After his death she came back, and has lived at home ever since.'

'It's surprising she's remained a widow. She must have been very fond of him.'

'She was when she married him, as I've told you.'

'Not afterwards?'

He shrugged. 'Susan's never told anyone she wasn't; she's too loyal. But anyone who knows her as well as I do gets to know things without being told. My idea is, she found out that he was skirt-mad, an absolute wolf. If she did I am sure she would have left him sooner or later. Susan's broadminded up to a point, but she isn't one to share her husband with every Anne, Jane, and Mary in the neighbourhood.'

His scowl did not surprise me. I had already discovered that he and his sister were extremely devoted to each other, just as they were to their parents. As I had suspected, Susan and her brother had some European blood in them: their maternal grandmother had been born in Marseilles.

The news that Susan's first marriage had been a near-failure encouraged me to propose marriage to her. To my great joy she accepted me. When I kissed her for the first time I knew I hadn't made a mistake. Her lips clung to mine; her arms were so tight round me I thought she intended never to release me again. Not that I wanted to be released. That evening I knew I was the happiest, and the luckiest, man in the world.

My parents liked her, too. They liked Edward: they liked Mr. and Mrs. Meredith. Susan and Anne liked each other at sight. In fact, everybody liked everybody else. It was almost too good to be true.

An idyllic month followed. I saw Susan most evenings, but not all: she had a job, as secretary, with one of the large corporations which are all too regrettably swallowing up smaller private concerns. Now and again she was asked to work overtime. Every time she 'phoned to tell me this I suffered qualms of conscience: it didn't seem right that Susan, bless her darling self, should be working while I lounged about with nothing to do but watch TV or go round to the pub. So, to ease my conscience, I worked too, trying to write a play. If Michael Gilbert could write plays in his spare time I didn't see why I couldn't do the same.

One evening Susan said:

'Darling, when are we going to be married?'

That is when it started.

2

H er expression shadowed. Had I not believed otherwise I should have taken it to be doubtful, even dismayed.

'Something wrong?' I asked.

'Wrong!'

I could see she was not with me. 'You should have seen the look on your face.'

'You should have seen the look on *your* face, darling, when I spoke of marriage.' Her eyes were solemn, questioning. 'Have you changed your mind? Don't you want to marry me?'

'Good God!' I exploded. 'What gave you that idea? I love you, Susan, I love you. That means marriage, doesn't it, in any civilized language?'

She relaxed with a tremulous sigh. 'For a moment I thought…' She shivered. 'What were you thinking, darling?'

It was my turn to be embarrassed. 'Of two things, I guess. To begin with, I was kicking myself for not having given a thought to the future, just because I have been too occupied in being supremely happy.'

She reached up to kiss me. 'Nice Iain,' she whispered in between kisses. 'And the other thing?'

'It's not easy to tell you this, but the thought flashed through my mind that I can't afford to marry you until I get a job. Of course, it shouldn't take me too long to find one but until I do…'

She looked at me with puzzled eyes. 'But you're a successful author, darling.'

I made a wry face at her. 'Successful, my eye! It's funny, but most people have the idea that, *a*, an author doesn't work, and, *b*, that he is automatically wealthy if he publishes books.'

'But you publish one book every year. I thought you made enough to live on.'

'Barely enough for one person to live on—living in somebody else's home.'

'Well then!' Her smile was enough to melt the heart of a dragon. 'I'm earning enough to keep me, and share the expenses of our home. What have we to worry about?'

'If you think you're going to carry on working once we are married—'

'Of course I shall,' she interrupted coolly. 'Don't be so old-fashioned, my darling. In these days many wives go out to work. They have to, for economic reasons.'

'Not in my family they don't.'

'There always has to be a first time. Now that that's settled...'

I was seeing Susan in a new light. She was normally so yielding. But I had a masterful nature, too.

'No,' I said stoutly. 'No, absolutely, no.'

We were married six weeks later. We had an ecstatic eighteen days' honeymoon. The remaining three days of Susan's three weeks' holiday we spent settling ourselves in our new home, a wedding present from my parents. The first Monday thereafter Susan went back to her job.

It seemed funny to see her off at the gate, to kiss her good-bye until six o'clock that night, to watch her disappear round the corner on her way to the Underground station. It seemed funny to return to the empty, silent house in the knowledge that I should be spending the next nine hours or so on my own. Funny, but not amusing. Good God! I reflected. If I'm not damned careful I'll be taking the washing round to the launderette for the sake of a half-hour's gossip!

Nor was it funny ha-ha to have to prepare one's own lunch. I stuck it for two days, with the help of a tin-opener. After that I arranged to have lunch with my mother most days of the week. For the rest; well, an author's life is normally a lonely one.

An idyllic year passed. We were so deuced happy, there were times when I wondered how long our happiness would last. I'm by way of being a pessimist where happiness is concerned, also a believer in the immutable law of averages. Sooner or later the arbiter of fate would wake up to the fact that Mr. and Mrs. Iain Carter were too happy: it wasn't fair to the rest of mankind: something must be done to bring them down to the norm of human existence. In spite of these fears, nothing happened to spoil our happiness. On the financial front we neither starved nor indulged in riotous living. Our joint income enabled us, with care, to live in moderate comfort, but no more—except for a holiday on the continent each year—a 'must' for a writer. To pay for it we both stopped smoking, and drank spirits only when we had guests.

We continued to see a lot of Edward; also our respective parents. One day, Edward was promoted, and celebrated his good luck—or his reward for hard work, whichever way you look at it—by proposing marriage to Anne. She promptly accepted him, so there was another marriage ceremony.

And then—well, it had to happen, I suppose.

'Darling,' Susan said to me one night, 'I've deceived you.'

I wasn't unduly alarmed. I had complete trust in her. Susan would never let anyone down, least of all anyone she loved.

'Tell me the gory details.'

'You remember my telling you I should be late coming home? I said nothing about staying at the office, did I?'

'No, but—'

'You see, I intended to visit a man—at his home.'

'Very well, give me his name and address. Tomorrow or the next day I'll shoot him, and give Edward some extra work to do. Mind you, I'll plead the thirteenth commandment.'

'I am not joking. I really did what I said. The address was seventeen Arcadia Avenue, and the name of the man was Dr. Charles Andrews.'

'Dr. Andrews!' I caught her to me. 'My God! What is wrong?'

She laughed. 'I've never seen anyone get in such a tizzy as you do, if you think I'm not well. Darling, please don't squeeze the breath out of me. It's not bad news.'

The slight emphasis on the final adjective was the clue. I let go of her and flopped into a chair. 'Good lord! You mean there's something in the oven?'

'Not the most elegant way of putting it, dearest, but that's exactly what I do mean.' She sat on my lap and cuddled up to me. 'Happy?'

'Give me a chance to absorb the news. When?'

'About the end of May.'

'A nice time to be born,' I remarked absentmindedly. I reflected for a few minutes. 'That settles it. This time I really will look for a job.'

'Why? I can take my summer holidays then.'

'No.' I was determined. 'No more office work for you once you become a mother.'

She was quiet for so long I wondered what she was thinking.

'Don't you like the idea?'

'I'm afraid I do, but how can I leave? We shall need the money more than ever.'

'Not if I take a job.'

She shook her head. 'It wouldn't be fair on you, darling, to ask you to give up writing. You love it too much.'

'I love writing. It's the only thing I want to do. But I needn't give it up. Other people have jobs and write too. Not more than a handful of novelists can live from writing books.'

'Are you sure we couldn't live on what you earn? Didn't your last book do better?'

'Thanks to selling in the U.S.A. and earning a thousand-dollar advance, yes. Even so...'

'How much do you earn per book?'

'Five thousand copies were printed. Last week there were only two hundred and fifty-five copies left.'

'Is that a good sale?'

'For somebody whose name isn't Agatha Christie, Ian Fleming, or John Creasey, it's not bad, especially now that I am earning twelve-and-a-half per cent to three thousand, and fifteen per cent thereafter.'

'If the book was published at fifteen shillings that means you earn...' She paused to work it out.

'Ninety-three pounds twelve shillings and sixpence per thousand copies at twelve-and-a-half per cent,' I supplied. I knew the figures by heart.

'Call it ninety pounds for convenience. Five times ninety is four hundred and fifty. But as you get an extra two-and-a-half per cent after three thousand five hundred—'

'Whoa! You go too fast. Authors get full royalties only on copies sold in the United Kingdom. On copies sold to the Dominions, Colonies, and overseas possessions, etc., instead of having twelve-and-a-half per cent on the retail price, we receive only ten per cent of the wholesale price, a difference, on a fifteen-shilling book, between one and tenpence halfpenny and, say, something under ninepence.'

In her indignation she sat up.

'That's not fair.'

'You're telling me.'

'Why?' she demanded. 'Do readers in Australia, New Zealand and so on pay less than we do?'

'On the contrary, I've been told they often pay more.'

'Then why do authors receive less?'

'It costs more in overheads, transport, and so on to send books to Australia; and Australian wholesalers say they have to buy more cheaply than British booksellers because it costs more to send copies to their retailers.'

'How many copies are sold overseas?'

'Nearly a third, I suppose—at any rate, initially.'

'So what will you earn on your last book?'

'Say about three thousand five hundred sold in U.K. That equals two hundred and eighty pounds odd on the first three thousand, and, say, fifty-six pounds odd on the remaining five hundred, or about three hundred and thirty-six pounds in all. The royalty on the overseas copies may come to about fifty pounds or thereabouts. That makes an approximate total of four hundred pounds per title, on English book sales.'

'And it takes you how long to write a book?'

'How long it takes to write a book isn't so important to the full-time, professional author. It is a question of how often a publisher will publish an author. The answer is nine months to a year—preferably a year in these days.'

'So the writer of a second-rank detective story or thriller is lucky to earn four to five hundred pounds a year?'

'Yes. And don't forget, I am earning more per book than some thriller writers, partly because Uncle James is my publisher, and is reasonably generous with his terms, partly because his travellers know I am his nephew and give my books that extra little push which enormously helps subscription sales. So you see, sweetheart, we can't raise a family on what I earn as a writer.'

'But some thriller writers make a lot of money. I was reading the other day about one author who earns thousands of pounds a year.'

'By writing under more than one name, darling. The majority of professional writers use more than one. They have to, to be able to live on their writing and not take a job.'

'Couldn't you use a second name instead of taking a job?'

That was the sixty-four-thousand-dollar question.

'How about John Ky. Lowell?'

Although this was the following evening, Susan knew what I meant. Her reaction was immediate and enthusiastic. 'Absolutely right, darling. John Ky. Lowell. It trips nicely off the tongue; a name anyone could remember.'

'But won't,' I retorted, prompted by my usual pessimism. 'Nobody I've met has ever heard the name of Iain Carter.'

'They will in time.' Susan is invariably optimistic. 'What does the "Ky" stand for? Sounds Siamese or something.'

'That's the idea. If I can find a wide-awake publisher he could make a gimmick of that question. Once you get people asking what Ky. with a full stop stands for, I'd be on my way to success.'

'Cynic!'

'Not really, darling. It is publicity which sells an author's books in these days, not what's printed inside.'

'Iain!' She was strangely excited.

'I'm listening.'

'Are you going to write detective stories under the new name?'

'Perhaps.'

'Why not write about police detectives for a change?'

'For a change! What am I doing at the moment?'

'I mean, realistic stories. Semi-documentaries.'

I laughed. 'My love, a dozen authors already publish so-called realistic books about police detectives. It's the current fashion. Private eyes are out of date.'

'"So-called" are the operative words. Have you read any?'

'A few.'

'Are they realistic?'

'Well—I might think so if I hadn't had the genuine lowdown from Edward.'

'That's the point I'm getting at. Why not make use of the material he's given to you?'

'God! He'd tear me limb from limb. His dope really is from the inside, off the record. If I weren't his brother-in-law...'

'Did he say anything about its being confidential?'

'No, but I'm damned sure that if it got back to his superiors that Edward's brother-in-law was the author of the kind of book you're thinking of there might be hell to pay. He might even be charged with an offence under the Official Secrets Act.'

'They will not find out if you use a nom-de-plume.'

I chuckled. 'Don't you believe it, my love. No publisher yet has ever succeeded in concealing the identity of a nom-de-plume, even when he has tried his best to.'

'If only the publisher himself knows!'

'Other people are bound to find out. The secretary who takes down his letters, the production department which sends out galley or page proofs for revision, the department responsible for preparing royalty statements, and so on. And, believe me, if the Press should ever become sufficiently interested to want the information, they'd nose it out soon enough. A few fivers are very useful in loosening tongues.'

For a moment she looked disappointed, but not for long. Once again she revealed animation. 'Suppose all business were conducted through a literary agent? Suppose the publisher didn't know the author's name was a nom-de-plume?'

'Wouldn't help much. Although the publisher's staff wouldn't be able to betray the identity of the author, the agent's employees could.'

She frowned. 'There must be some way of protecting a secret.'

'If a government staff can't! The vital information that leaks out!'

'Suppose you were to write a story about an author who wanted to conceal his nom-de-plume, how would you make him do so?'

Crafty little minx! I grinned, and began to reflect. Presently:

'To begin with, I would make the author type his own manuscripts instead of sending them out to a typing agency, and that's a bind to begin with. Retyping, I mean.'

She nodded. 'Yes, I can see that, but his wife would do his typing for him.'

'If the secret is to be kept? Be your age, darling.'

She pinched me. 'And you be a gentleman for once, by admitting that a woman can keep a secret, when it is necessary, as much as any man can.'

'I'll admit that *you* can, sweetheart.'

She smiled at me, kissed me. 'Nice husband,' she murmured. 'Right, the script has been written, revised, and retyped. What next?'

'It is sent to a literary agent—'

'You said agents were out.'

'Wait for it! With the script goes a letter to say that the author cannot give an address in England to write to because he lives abroad, and is always travelling here, there, and everywhere.'

'Ah!'

'The letter goes on to say something like this: "Should your readers advise you to handle the rights of this book would you please do so forthwith, without further instructions from me, and insert an advertisement in the Personal Column of the *Daily Telegraph* on the first Friday of the subsequent month, addressed to Lit. Opt., to say that you are handling the script—or alternatively, that you do not see your way to. For the cost of this, and possibly other advertisements, I enclose a five-pound note." Get the idea, darling?'

She nodded. 'Of course. And when the story is sold—'

'If.'

'When,' she repeated firmly. 'He will advertise: "Have sold story. Where shall I send contract to?"'

'Exactly right.'

'And where do you tell him to send the contract to?' she asked sweetly. 'To Iain Carter, Esq., of three, Hampshire Crescent!'

I sighed. 'Nobody gives me credit for genuine intelligence, not even my wife. No, my sweet, to Monsieur Roger Phillips, or some other name, Poste Restante, at Cooks or one of the Paris Bureaux de Poste.'

'But if you ask someone to collect it for you that will mean somebody else sharing your secret.'

'Who said anything about somebody else collecting it? Paris is only an hour's flight from London.'

'Iain Carter, if you think I am going to let you loose in Paris…' She paused abruptly, whereupon I grinned. I had lived with her long enough to read her expression, and to know the way her mind works. 'Of course,' she added reflectively, 'there's no reason for your going on your own.' Her expression lit up. 'Do you know, darling, I am beginning to think there is something to be said for your scheme.' Then she gripped my hand, hard. 'Oh!'

'Now what?'

'Does a foreigner have to show his passport to collect Poste Restante letters?'

'Might be.'

'Well, then? Your passport is in the name of Carter, not Phillips.'

'So what! Ever heard Edward talk of the man Dutchy, of Frith Street?'

'Isn't he a criminal the police have been after for years without being able to pull in, for lack of evidence?'

'That's the type. He'll supply a fake passport—for a price.'

She stared at me with admiration. 'No wonder your plots are noted for their ingenuity. What a good thing you are not a crook.

But now, you have collected the contract, signed and returned it. What next?'

'There's not much more to worry about. I'll give the agent instructions to handle all negotiations without reference to me.'

'What about correcting proofs? Does that mean another visit to Paris? A nice idea, but a little expensive. And if the idea is to make money...'

'I'll not worry about correcting proofs, unless we need an excuse to go to Paris. There are advertisers in *The Bookseller, Books and Bookmen*, etc., who revise scripts or correct proofs for a fee. I'll instruct the agent to have proofs sent to one.'

After a long pause she nodded. 'It does seem possible. What about money? How is the agent to pay you that? Send a cheque to Paris?'

'The money aspect is the most difficult problem of the lot, sweetheart. Obviously, a cheque is out of the question. If it is made out to me, bang goes the anonymity. If it is made out to John Ky. Lowell, the people in the bank would know who Lowell is, and although all bank staffs are sworn to secrecy...' I shrugged. 'Somebody might let it out quite innocently, without giving the matter a thought, not knowing the importance of concealing the real identity of John Ky. Lowell. But we'll worry about the question of money when we come to it.'

She squeezed my hand. 'Then you're going to?'

'It's become a challenge, and you know how much I like to prove myself cleverer than the bloke next door...'

Filled with enthusiasm, I started work on the new book which, I hoped, would ultimately be the first of a series by John Ky. Lowell. My original conception of the plot starred a divisional C.I.D. man by the ordinary name of Smith—William Bertie Smith, detective-superintent, Q division. Smith was to be the 'hero' of the series; a hard-cussing, fault-finding disciplinarian, heartily disliked by every man who served with him because of his sheer, unhuman efficiency; a man with the brain of an electronic computor. Naturally, he was to solve every case with which he should become connected, during the course of which he would expose the secrets of police investigation, and introduce a number of thinly disguised genuine members of the Metropolitan Police Force.

Within a few days of beginning, a mysterious thing happened to me. But perhaps I had better explain that an author's consciousness does not work as smoothly and obediently as many people believe. Some, though not all, characters begin to dominate him, rather than the reverse. They ultimately possess him by creating their own characteristics, dictating their own movements, inventing their own habits. Creatures of the subconscious, they are conceived and grow in spite of, not because of, him.

Before I had written two chapters, William Bertie Smith was dominating me. What was worse, he was proving to be completely different from the man his embryo had destined him to be. He was hard-cussing, yes. Fault-finding, too; but never for justifiable reasons. As the saying goes, he could not see the wood for the trees. He would bully a subordinate for spelling the verb *practise* with a 'c' instead of an 's', and remain completely oblivious of the fact that the man had forgotten to make a note of the registration number of a car involved in a smash-and-grab raid. If there were two suspects in a crime it became a certainty for him to suspect the innocent one, and so waste valuable time in finding that out. Where he was concerned, intuition (that invaluable 5 per cent asset in the good detective's make-up) was completely missing. As for his electronic computing ability, it invariably made two and two add up to five. In short he was completely inefficient—but lucky. God, how lucky! 'Lucky Smith' his fellow detectives called him. Never mind how many mistakes he made, or how badly he conducted an investigation, luck always came to his aid. Not 5 per cent luck in his case, but 55 per cent, or more. That is why he became a superintendent—that, and the fact that he was a nephew of the commissioner.

Perhaps P. G. Wodehouse is the villain, he and his incomparable Bertie Wooster. Maybe if I had never read Wodehouse my subconscious would never have dreamed up W. B. Smith.

But there it was. W. B. Smith having taken possession of me, and having created himself, as it were, there was nothing more I could do about it, unless I brought about a miscarriage by tearing up all I had written (four chapters by then) and starting afresh. I didn't have the courage to do that.

Something else happened to me. I had started to write the book with the deliberate intention of producing a commercial product, a saleable book which would be sufficiently conventional to appeal to non-critical readers of commercial and public libraries. After all, I should soon be needing the few hundred pounds I hoped it would bring in.

Unfortunately, that mischievous subconscious of mine had other ideas. Before I realized what was happening I found myself writing a vitriolic satire. Set with the problem of arresting and charging the murderer of Sally Underwood, W. B. Smith and his team conduct the investigation with an elephantine heaviness that metaphorically tramples underfoot, one by one, five clues palpably indicating the identity of the murderer.

I knew very well that I was caricaturing the pompous, dictatorial superintendent, that there wasn't a reader from John o' Groats to Land's End who would believe in the existence of this larger-than-life congenital idiot, but the story fascinated me. I knew I was writing the best book I would ever write. I knew also that the chances of having it published were a thousand to one against. If there was one canon of conventional detective-story writing the story didn't ignore and spurn, then I knew nothing about detective stories and hadn't learned a thing about writing books.

'And you suggested my writing a realistic story!' I threw the chapters down on the table with an angry gesture. 'Damn and blast the ruddy thing!'

'Isn't it going well, darling?'

'Just disastrously, that's all.'

'How far have you got?'

'Finished the tenth chapter this afternoon.'

'Why go on with it?'

'Because I love it, Susan dear. I'm enjoying every word. It's more than a bloody good story, it's brilliant, I'm a ruddy genius, but I'm wasting my time. The damn' thing can't sell. No publisher in his sane senses would dream of publishing it.'

'Why?'

'Why! You've read it to date, haven't you?'

'Yes, dearest, every word. It's a superbly written story. But'—she grimaced—'to begin with, I don't know what Superintendent Waller will say if he reads it.'

I stared at her. 'Why should he have anything to say? Not that he will ever read it.'

'My, you are in a tizzy tonight. Why not have a drink?'

'I don't want a drink. I don't need a drink. I don't—'

'I'd like one.'

I was instantly contrite. I poured out two sherries, swallowed mine at a gulp. 'What about Waller?'

'Just that he's your Superintendent W. B. Smith.'

'He's what! Don't be silly, sweetheart. A real Smith wouldn't exist five minutes in the Force.'

'Of course, you've exaggerated him, but from what Edward has told us from time to time I am sure you used Waller as a prototype for Superintendent Smith.'

I groaned. 'I didn't realize that. The tricks one's subconscious can get up to.'

'But yours is a very clever subconscious.' She sat on the edge of my chair and played with my hair. 'I get so annoyed with the Superintendent for overlooking the obvious I want to smack him, to shake him out of his terrifying complacency. He is a wonderful character, darling; so real, so alive, even if he is less a detective than a—than—than an undetective.'

'An undetective! Ye gods! That's it! The title! *The Undetective.*' In my enthusiasm I pulled her down on my lap and kissed her until she was breathless.

I finished the book, revised and retyped it. Susan was still working at the office. Then I sent it off to one of the leading literary agents and waited for the verdict to appear in the *Daily Telegraph*—though not with any feeling of either impatience or excitement. I knew it had enough merit to warrant its being offered. To the last line I had continued to believe it to be a fine novel, however unusual. Neither revision, time, nor afterthoughts caused me to change this opinion. But whether it would sell...

Sure enough, one Friday morning an announcement in the

personal column informed me that the agents would offer the script to publishers. What I had to do next was to wait patiently for the next announcement to say that the story had been sold. This could easily take several months, unless it were accepted at first or second offering. Publishers take up to two months to reject some books in these days; a warning to any newcomer to the ranks of would-be novelists that he needs long patience, and an even longer pocket; he will be lucky if he sees his book in print within nine months of acceptance.

In May, as promised, Susan produced a son and heir; though an heir to what was a matter for conjecture. My balance at the bank was fast diminishing. There might or might not be a modicum of reason in the old fairy story that two can live as cheaply as one—but add a baby and see what happens!

In June the following advertisement appeared in the *Telegraph*:

Lit. Opt. Happy announce sale. Send address soonest possible for agreement and the cheque. A. B. Wen & Son.

'It's been accepted, darling. It's been accepted.' Now I was excited. I went dancing into the kitchen.

'*The Undetective*?'

'Yes.'

Floury hands and all, she hugged me. 'Oh, Iain!' She drew back, smiled into my face. 'I knew somebody would want it.'

'You knew...' I gasped. 'I like that. It was you who said W. B. Smith couldn't detect the smell of fish at Billingsgate. It was you who gave it its title.'

'That didn't mean I didn't have faith in it—unlike its creator.'

'I didn't, did I? Come to that, I still don't think it will sell well.'

She laughed until she cried. 'I've never met such a pessimist, darling. Why shouldn't it sell well if it's a good book—which it is?'

'Because the public like their detectives to be detectives, not undetectives.'

'Perhaps, but when readers realize how clever the book is, how thrilling the plot is, how authentic the police procedure is—they won't have to be told that it is, they will sense that for themselves—they'll take to it, see if they don't.'

I grinned. 'From which I gather you think my book is reasonably good?'

She didn't reply, but said 'Oh!' in such a dismal voice I wondered what had happened. When she showed me her hands I did some detective work, and deduced the fact that the back of my dark-grey jacket was in somewhat of a mess.

Happily unaware of the dramatic consequences which were to come from my semi-light-hearted frolic to create a water-tight nom-de-plume for myself, I set into operation the next stage in my plan. I telephoned a certain Gerrard number.

A deep husky voice answered the ring.

'Yes.'

'Is that Franz Schmidt, otherwise Dutchy to his pals?'

'Yes.'

'I'm told by a chum of mine that you are very good at supplying passports for people who haven't the—er—time to apply to the proper department.'

'It's a lie, mister. Who told you?'

'No names, no pack drill, but I have faith in that pal's word, see. Do you think you would have faith in it, too, if I were to send you an envelope with ten old pound notes in it tomorrow morning?'

'It's a lie, by Gott! I tell you—'

'Fifteen, then?'

'Don't bother me, I'm a busy man.'

'How much does it cost to have faith in one's fellow human beings?'

'Funny guy, heh!' A slight pause. 'Twenty-five punt could make me a goot Christian.'

'Can't afford more than twenty.'

'Twenty-two punt ten.'

It was my turn to pause. £22 10s.! Exactly 25 per cent of what I was likely to receive as an advance on account of royalties, after the agent had deducted his 10 per cent commission.

'Make it twenty, Dutchy,' I pleaded. 'I'm hard up.'

'All right,' he unexpectedly agreed. 'Send me twenty punt, all particulars, and a photo. Where shall I send it, when I've collected it?'

A photograph! Where to send the faked passport? Two minor problems to which I hadn't given a thought. I reflected quickly.

'I'll give you the address with the photo.'

'Okay, mister, but don't play no funny tricks if you see what I mean. It won't get you nowhere. I ain't promised nodding.'

I did see what he meant. If my message were a police trap he would deny everything, say he thought I wanted him to act merely as messenger. Hence his caution in emphasizing the fact that he would 'collect' the passport. As for the amount involved, well, a man's time was valuable, wasn't it? and worth what anyone else was willing to pay for it.

From the public telephone box, which I had been careful to use, I went to Fleet Street, where I inserted the following advertisement in the *Evening News*:

Despairing author wants well-paid editorial position in publisher's office. No previous experience, but willing to learn. Box No.—

The advertisement was accepted with bland indifference. 'Box number 20A13,' I was told. 'Will you collect any replies, or shall we forward them?'

I said I would collect and passed over the sum demanded.

I went on to a photographer in the Strand, who specialized in taking passport photographs. A dark-haired man wearing a white-spotted bow-tie and Italian shoes glanced enquiringly at me.

'Can you take a photograph of me that nobody could possibly recognize as me?' I asked.

'You mean a passport photograph, sir,' he said without a smile. He thought I was joking. 'Will you step in there?'

I sat down. He began to switch on lights. 'I mean what I said about not being recognized,' I told him. 'I want to play a practical joke on a friend.'

'I'll do my best.' He studied me. 'Just a question of lighting.'

As a passport photographer the man was a genius. I collected the photographs some hours later. I could barely recognize myself. I had no fear that Dutchy might one day accidentally spot me in the street, and follow me home with the idea of possibly blackmailing me.

This fear was not exaggerated. Edward had spoken often enough of the criminal fraternity. Once let them suspect you of having a secret, and they will ferret it out for their own nefarious purposes.

I sent the photographs, the £20, false particulars of myself in the name of Roger Phillips, and the *Evening News* box number, to Franz Schmidt.

Later, I returned to Fleet Street to collect the passport. To my astonishment I found, not the solitary packet from Dutchy, but five envelopes in all.

A little worried, I opened them in turn. The first came from a publisher in Torquay whose name I had never heard of. He offered to publish my books at my own expense which, he explained in tempting language, would mean my receiving not only the normal royalties, but also a substantial share of publisher's profits.

The second and third letters were from unknown literary agents, who guaranteed to transform me from a despairing into a jubilant author.

The fourth letter came from a firm of Golders Green tailors who claimed that my failure to succeed as a writer was obviously due to my not wearing the right clothes. If I would care to call at their High Class Tailoring Establishment...

The fifth and last envelope contained the passport. Mr. John Ky. Lowell, alias Roger Phillips, had come into existence.

In the past I had never worried about passing through Customs, either at home or abroad. Because I had never tried to smuggle anything through, my innocence had acted like a charm. No Customs officers had ever troubled to rummage through my luggage. No more than a cursory glance and, hey presto, I was through.

Gone was that enviable sensation of unconcern. On my way to Dover I was haunted by the knowledge that I was carrying two passports on me. I kept dabbing my upper lip and my forehead with my handkerchief, to make sure I was not sweating, a physical and psychological manifestation which immediately arouses the suspicions of a Customs officer the world over. Hence the reason for keeping Customs-examination sheds icy cold; to make sure that the sweating is brought about by guilty conscience, not natural warmth.

As the train passed through Tonbridge I decided to prepare myself for all eventualities, and invent a story to account for having a second passport in my possession, just in case one of the officers took it into his head to search my person.

By the time we reached Ashford I had my story pat. Long before we reached Folkestone I had completely recovered my self-possession.

Having shown my own passport I went through Dover Customs without arousing in the officer even the semblance of interest in me and my possessions. But half-way to the French coast a reflection disturbed me. If I were to make use of the Phillips passport by showing it to Poste Restante clerks it was necessary to have it date-stamped by the French immigration officials. The prospect of having to show it to security men caused me to sweat once more. Because it was essential to transfer the two passports I plucked up courage to go downstairs to a lavatory and, hidden from curious eyes, exchanged my own passport for the false one, extracted from an inside pocket.

I need not have worried. Neither the French immigration officials nor Douane seemed interested in me. I reached Paris without trouble, and having booked a room in a small hotel near the Gare du Nord, I telephoned Messrs. A. B. Wen's in London.

The connection was soon made. I asked for Mr. Arthur Wen, and gave the girl my pseudonym. A few minutes later I heard a deep, rather pleasant voice.

'Mr. Lowell, I am delighted to have this opportunity of speaking to you. I understand from my secretary that you are telephoning from Paris, so I must not keep you talking too long. But please allow me to say how much pleasure your script gave me when I read it. Most amusing, and most instructive. I was delighted when I sold it to the first publisher to whom I sent it. You will find that Cassins are a first-class firm, real live wires, and Jack Cassins an excellent fellow, an excellent fellow.'

'I am glad to hear it. My grateful thanks to you, Mr. Wen, for your interest in my effort.'

'Not at all, not at all. Now to business. The contract is ready for your signature. You may take it from me that the terms are generous for a first novel, yes, generous. Jack Cassins is determined to make a success of you, and wishes to attract and hold your goodwill. Where shall I send it to?'

'To Roger Phillips—perhaps I should explain that John Ky. Lowell is a pseudonym.'

'Quite so, quite so.'

'To Roger Phillips, c/o Cooks and Wagon-Lits, rue Royale, Paris.'

'Ah, yes! I know the place. On a corner site, opposite the Madeleine.'

'That's it.'

'And the money? I am pleased to tell you that Cassins has agreed an advance of one hundred and fifty pounds, half of which is payable forthwith.'

'Good. Would you please arrange to send the equivalent in French francs to Westminster Bank, in Place Vendôme, payable against identification.'

'Certainly, Mr. Lowell—or shall I call you Mr. Phillips?'

'Whichever you prefer.'

'Then I shall stick to Mr. Lowell. I have great hopes that Lowell will become quite a well-known name in the course of time. Yes, I shall arrange that right away. Would you like the money telegraphed?'

'Please. I have to leave Paris very soon. Must be in Rome by the end of the week.'

'Leave everything to me, sir. We are used to sending money to authors in all parts of the world. Shall I send any further communications care of Cooks?'

'No. I may prefer you to write to me in Brussels, at Lyons, Madrid—well, one never knows. I am prepared to leave all negotiations entirely in your hands, and to accept your judgment, in which I have complete faith.'

'You are very kind, Mr. Lowell, very kind. I appreciate your trust.'

'If you wish to contact me urgently, an advertisement in the Personal Column of the *Daily Telegraph* will warn me to telephone you. Regular royalty statements can be sent to Westminster Bank, to await arrival, unless you hear from me to the contrary.'

'As you say, as you say.'

And there, save for a few politenesses, the conversation ended.

*

Three days later I called at Cooks, and asked if there was a letter
for Roger Phillips. There was. A charming one from Arthur Wen,
enclosing the contract and informing me that the money had been
telegraphed to Paris as instructed.

I signed and returned the contract, then walked to Place Vendôme.
At the Westminster Bank I had no difficulty in collecting a nice wad
of crisp, new notes, the French equivalent of £75, less 10 per cent
commission, less income tax at standard rate.

From Place Vendôme I walked up the rue de la Paix to Place de
l'Opéra, where I entered the branch there of the Crédit Lyonnais. To
a bland member of the staff I handed over the francs, and in halting
French made known the fact that I wished to open a bank account
in the name of Deekes Wendell. There was no difficulty, just a few
formalities.

Then I telephoned my French literary agent.

'Monsieur Paul Peugeot?'

'*Oui, monsieur.*'

'This is Deekes Wendell speaking, of Fifth Avenue, New York,'
I said quickly, speaking English with what I fondly hoped was a slight
American accent. 'I have just come from England, where I met an
English author by the name of Iain Carter. I understand you are his
French agent.'

'But yes, Monsieur Wendell, I have that privilege.' Peugeot's
English was infinitely better than my American.

'Then listen, monsieur. Back in the States I run a syndication
agency for the sale of serial rights throughout the English-speaking
world. I have been reading Iain Carter's books and think they stand a
chance of selling here, there, and wherever. For reasons concerning
nobody but myself I normally have cash funds available in Europe
which are more convenient for me to pay to English and European
authors than deal with U.S. and Canadian dollars, Australian pounds
and so on. Do you follow me?'

'Perfectly, monsieur.'

I grinned. I was quite sure he did. Trust a Frenchman to sympathize with anyone juggling with the intricacies of foreign exchanges. I didn't doubt he had already decided I was up to some form of jiggery-pokery, but if it meant paying less income tax here, there, and other places, the best of luck to me.

'Right. Mr. Carter has suggested that I should pay to you, to hold on his behalf, any moneys that may be owing to him from time to time, you to remit these to him when you send him statements of French sales, which you do twice a year, when there's anything to report.'

'That is so, monsieur. Each February and August.'

'Mr. Carter tells me he does not wish you to incur any expenses in doing this kindness to us both, and suggests you deduct a five per cent commission from all moneys you remit to him from syndication sales.'

'That is very generous on Monsieur Carter's part, monsieur.' Peugeot's voice was strangely affable. 'It will give me much pleasure to do this service for him.'

'Excellent, then that's all settled. The money will reach you at irregular intervals, according to when I can come to Paris. I'll give you a ring now and again. Now, if you will excuse me, I must catch the 'plane for New York—'

'Monsieur Wendell, one moment, please.' His voice sounded anxious.

'Sure, what is it?'

'May I have the privilege of sending you books by some of the other English authors I represent in France?'

Trust a canny Frenchman never to miss a trick! I cursed his bright business instinct. 'I'll take that up with you the next time I 'phone. Glad to have spoken with you, monsieur.'

'Always at your service, monsieur. *Au revoir* and *bon voyage…*'

4

I t happens sometimes, perhaps more often than we think, that luck plays a large part in achieving success for a particular book. It is a question of timing. If a book based on the death of a fictional Prime Minister should be published about the time of death of a real Prime Minister, the betting is ten to one on the book's receiving an extraordinary amount of extra publicity—and everyone connected with the literary profession knows that it is publicity which often creates the best-seller, not necessarily the excellence of its writing. An alternative to coincidence lies in the author's playing the principle rôle in a divorce case or other scandalous proceedings.

For this reason I do not claim credit for the extraordinary success of *The Undetective*. For so long had the national Press been emphasizing the public's slackening confidence and faith in the English police forces that the general public, brain-washed by repetitious criticism, had fallen victim to the latest fad: that of substituting for individual reasoning the lazier habit of agreeing with mass opinion. So everybody found fault with the police and eagerly read my book.

It is true that the police had had an unfortunate period immediately preceding its publication. They had failed (as far as was generally known) in solving the death of two teen-age girls on Wimbledon Common. There had been five bank and seven sub-post-office robberies in three weeks. In that same period five wage-grabs had reached a total of more than £60,000 stolen. Besides these more recent crimes there was a twelve-month back-log of unsolved cases which the newspapers repeated *ad nauseam*.

On the credit side of police activities more cars than ever before had been towed away from their parking places: more motorists had paid £2 parking fines: more motorists had been charged with speeding and other road-traffic offences. As the newspapers claimed, a robber stood more chance of going unpunished for his crime than the unfortunate, long-suffering motorist.

For this reason, critics and newspaper crime reporters alike eagerly welcomed *The Undetective*. After the critics had given it ungrudging praise as a first-class novel the crime reporters went on to use it as another weapon in their word-war against the unfortunate police.

To Susan's and my delight the book reached the bestseller lists, whereupon it was bought by an American publisher. The first impression having sold in the first four weeks, a second in the next three, and a third in the next four, a fourth impression was put in hand. It was about this time that the *Daily Express* began to use the word *undetective* as an expression of scorn. 'Living up to their reputation as undetectives, so far the C.I.D. have failed to make any progress in their investigations…'

Two days later: 'Even the stupidest undetective should have realized…'

A week later: 'According to Mr. Jones's account, his first visitor was an undetective…'

My word—no, Susan's word, bless her darling heart—had passed into the English language.

The next three years passed like a dream. Susan produced a girl, Lindy, to keep her elder brother, Robert Iain, company. It was fortunate for us all that John Ky. Lowell was on hand to pay the bills.

By now William Bertie Smith was an established character; nearly as famous, in his own way, as James Bond, Maigret, Poirot, and Philip

Marlowe. The words undetective and undetection were in common usage. So were many other *uns*. Although Lewis Carroll had long since written of an Unbirthday, and a book had been published for ungardeners, it had been left to me to establish un as a contemptuous prefix for almost any noun.

'Come on, you ruddy unsoldiers, pick 'em up,' roared the sergeant on the parade-ground.

In an Ealing District train a man was heard to say miserably: 'Fillet steak at home! And waste hard-earned money! Not me; my wife's an uncook. Shepherd's pie is about her best.'

A critic in the *Sunday Times:* 'As an unactor, Anders Anderson achieves the summit of his unart.'

Another critic, in the *Manchester Evening News:* 'In contrast with the authors reviewed above, Iain Carter is a typical unwriter. He has obviously read that master of satirical detection, John Ky. Lowell, too well and not wisely, and his *Prelude for Supposition* is a poor imitation of the master's *Never be Realistic.'*

And then somebody wrote to the *Daily Mirror.* 'Reference to the novelist, John Ky. Lowell, what is Ky. short for?' I suspect that the writer, Richard W. Bethell, was a member of the publisher's staff.

A few days later a headline in the *Daily Mirror:* 'Who is John Ky. Lowell?'

That was the beginning of a great hunt. Confronted with a mystery that was not immediately solvable at first attempt, editors of the popular Press became exasperated, and began to issue ultimatums. 'Dig out something about this man Lowell, or else!'

I am sure that Messrs. A. B. Wen & Son must have begun to curse the mystery of their client's identity; in spite of the money they were making from the increasing sale of translation and other subsidiary rights, both home and abroad. The reporters left Mr. Arthur Wen no peace.

'Who's this guy?' they demanded.

'John Ky. Lowell.'

'Is that his real name or a nom-de-plume?'

'I don't know.'

'Nuts! 'Course you do. You're his agent, aren't you?'

'Yes.'

'Well, then, give.'

'I tell you, I don't know what his real name is. I haven't seen his birth certificate.'

'Ever seen him?'

'No.'

'You write to him, don't you?'

'Of course.'

'Where does he live? What's his address?'

'I don't know.'

'Where do you write to?'

'Poste Restante, Paris, Brussels, The Hague, Le Touquet, where would you. He's always travelling.'

'What is he, besides being a writer?'

'I don't know.'

'You don't know much, do you? Is John Ky. Lowell the nom-de-plume of an established writer? John Creasey, for instance? He writes under half a dozen names already; one more or less wouldn't make any difference to him.'

'If Creasey is Lowell, he's never told me.'

In spite of their unwillingness to believe Mr. Wen, the reporters eventually conceded that they were wasting their time, and thereafter left him in peace.

Then, one day, I realized that I had created a Frankenstein monster that could easily destroy me, as a writer, if the secret of Lowell's identity were revealed. And not only me...

*

'Any idea who John Ky. Lowell is?' Edward asked.

We were sitting either side of a blazing fire. Susan was up with the children. Edward was smoking his pipe, a sign that he was relaxed and feeling content with life.

'Why?'

'He's storing up trouble for himself.'

'Trouble! How?'

'You've read the newspapers lately, haven't you?'

'All that nonsense about Lowell? The theory he's an ex-C.I.D. man?'

'Yes.'

I shrugged. 'They'll be off on a new tack next week.'

'Shouldn't be surprised. But Scotland Yard won't.'

'Scotland Yard!' His words shook me. 'What's Lowell to do with them?'

'To start with, he's got under the skin of the big boys at Central because he's making the C.I.D. a laughing-stock. They admit he's doing it in the nicest possible way, but just now the police are in need of good publicity, not satire. If the man has any sense he'll ease off on his ruddy William Bertie Smith.'

I was surprised at the extent of Edward's annoyance. I knew he was proud of the C.I.D., especially of the division he was in, but to be quite so het up...

'How am I supposed to know who he is?'

'That club you belong to, the one I gave a lecture to a year ago—'

'The Crime Writers' Association.'

He nodded. 'You meet every month, and I'll eat my hat if you ever talk about anything that isn't connected with books, publishing, and yourselves...'

I chuckled. 'Bang on. We don't.'

'Then don't tell me none of you has never dragged Lowell into the conversation.'

'I won't because I can't. They're just as keen as the newspapers are to know who he is.'

'Any suspicions?'

'Of course. John Creasey is the chief suspect, but he's given us his word he isn't. After him, Maurice Proctor, because of his one-time connection with the police. Some think Michael Gilbert is guilty, some think Michael Underwood is, because they're both lawyers. Others have suggested Ernest Dudley, Bernard Newman—well, think of every thriller writer you've heard of, and there's your answer. In fact, some of the members wonder whether Lowell is a double pseudonym, as it were, and that she's a woman; Margery Allingham, Ngaio Marsh, or Josephine Bell, for instance.'

Edward shook his head. 'You can kill that theory,' he asserted with decision.

'Why?'

'Lowell knows too much about the police to be a woman.'

'What about a policewoman?'

He looked surprised, ruffled his hair, and sucked away at his foul pipe. 'Could be,' he admitted. 'But I don't think so. I'd bet a fiver that the writer's a man. There's something about his viewpoint that pins a male label on him.'

'In that case, what about me? One critic accused me of trying to imitate John Ky. Lowell's style.'

He shook his head. 'I know you too well, Iain, old boy. You're too happy-going, too good-natured, to be a successful satirist. Besides, take his plots. A man would need to have the mind of a criminal, or a detective, to invent Lowell's type of devilishly ingenious story. But you're lucky not to be Lowell.'

'Good lord, why? He must be making a mint.'

'I'm trying to tell you why. Central is after his blood. If he is a member of the Force, he's for the high jump, p.b.q. If he's an ex-member, well, they're keeping quiet about what they'll do to him.'

'What can they do?'

Edward gestured aimlessly. 'One would have to know every damn' statute from the time of William the Conqueror onwards to answer that, but they'll dig out some old act that hasn't been repealed, you can be sure of that, and then they'll throw the book at him.'

'And if he isn't an ex.?'

'They'll throw it at the man who's feeding him the inside dope.'

That's what I mean about the Frankenstein monster. I had created the nom-de-plume as a gimmick, in a spirit of mischief, just for the fun of mystifying Nosy Parkers, and creating publicity. I had succeeded all too well. Now I daren't ever let it become known that I was John Ky. Lowell. Apart from consequences to myself, Edward would suffer, and through Edward, my own sister; to say nothing of Susan, and Edward's parents and my parents. And my children... My God! there was no end to the list.

As far as the Press was concerned the mystery of Lowell's identity ceased to be of any further interest. Newspapers do not waste time flogging a dead horse. A nine days' wonder means just that. Within that period of time every conceivable aspect of a sensation is normally unearthed, exaggerated, dramatized, publicized, criticized. Then it disappears, to await resurrection at the least excuse.

But in the literary world the subject continued to be absorbing, as I learned the next time I attended a meeting of the Crime Writers' Association. For the benefit of anyone who has never heard of the Association, and there may be a few people who have not, I should explain that it is an association of authors who write books in which crime is the *raison d'être*, either from the point of view of pure detection, suspense, or thrilling action. We meet once a month, about 5.30 p.m., and in a spirit of good comradeship and vague envy, with a glass in our hands, we talk about books and authors, or sometimes listen to lectures on precious stones, safes, forensic medicine, and so on.

On this occasion we just talked about books and authors, about ourselves, and especially about John Ky. Lowell. We also welcomed two members of our sister association in the U.S.A., the Mystery Writers of America, who were visiting this country. One way and another time passed quickly. With the clock approaching 7 p.m. members began to disappear.

For once I was in no particular hurry to leave, for Susan, having parked the children with her mother for the night, was not due home until eight-thirty. I ordered a last gin-and-mixed, but swallowed it at a gulp when T. C. H. Jacobs and Colin Robertson made a move towards the door.

'Coming, Iain?' said Jacques.

I looked round. Only Ernest Dudley, Margot Bennett, and Leo Harris, *Books & Bookmen* critic, were left, deep in conversation. Talking about books, I shouldn't wonder.

'Coming,' I answered.

The Armchair Detective saw me leaving and waved. I waved back.

'Couldn't be him, I suppose,' Jacques mused.

I knew what Jacques meant—Jacques being T. C. H. Jacobs to the rest of the world. So did Colin, apparently.

'He gets around, does our Ernest,' he joined in as we left Overseas House. 'And yet!'

'Exactly,' agreed Jacques. 'I'm not so sure that Lowell is the pseudonym of an established writer.'

'What do you think he is? A Scotland Yard man?

'He might well be, the way his books read. I thought I knew quite a bit about police procedure, but not to the extent Lowell does. Personally, I shouldn't be surprised to hear one day that he's a con man, or a master crook.'

'A master crook!' Colin jeered.

'All right, call them crime organizers, if you want to. You don't imagine the recent series of train robberies, and big hold-ups, were pulled off without a hell of a lot of damn' smart organizing?'

'But why a con man, say, rather than a detective?' I asked Jacques.

'Because of the way his mind works in planning his crimes: his meticulous attention to detail down to the nth degree, his allowance for every foreseeable complication, the scrupulous timing, and so on: the kind of brain a successful strategist must possess.'

'Maybe he's an ex-general.'

Colin chuckled. 'Not Monty, I hope?'

Jacques shook his head as we turned into Piccadilly. 'Monty wouldn't hide behind a pseudonym. He'd say what he wanted to say, and to hell with everyone.'

'So you think it's the fear of revealing his real identity and not just a publicity-gimmick that's made Lowell hide himself away?'

'Don't you? It's not natural to dislike publicity so much without good reason. Don't forget, in these days publicity means lolly.'

'Eden Phillpotts shunned publicity, and he had nothing to hide.'

'True, but he didn't conceal his identity, and keep his address secret even from his literary agent.'

'No,' I agreed. I pulled on my gloves. 'Wind's turning colder,' I said.

As I let myself into the house I reflected how cheerless it was to return to an empty home, not to be greeted by a living soul, welcomed with a kiss, or clutching, sticky fingers. The silence was so dismal. I became depressed, and hurried into the front room to switch on the radio. Even the hum of the valves warming up was comforting. A few moments later the welcome grandeur of a symphony filled the room: the B.B.C. Symphony Orchestra were playing Beethoven's Seventh. I increased the volume, switched on every light in the room, pulled the curtains, and set a match to the log fire. Although Mr. John Ky. Lowell had generously installed central heating for me, I refused to deprive myself of the cheerfulness of a fire.

Susan wasn't due back for another hour, so I gave myself a whisky-and-soda and lit a cigarette. Even if I was to be bored with my own company for a time, there was no reason why I shouldn't make myself comfortable.

But during that vital hour something happened that was to affect the lives of several people, not least of all myself.

A man named Alex Naughton was murdered.

5

' O h dear!' exclaimed Susan as she returned to the bedroom the following morning, reading the morning paper.
'I doubt whether we shall see anything of Edward for the next
few days.'

'Why not?'

'A man named Alex Naughton has been murdered in Cumberland
Road.'

I whistled. Cumberland Road was a little less than a mile away
from our home; well within the district under the control of the
division of which Edward was a member.

'That doesn't necessarily mean Edward will be drawn in. He
and Superintendent Waller are busy on the Barclays Bank robbery.'

'They're not, you know. When Edward telephoned yesterday
morning he said they'd cracked that case and were charging four
men within the hour. They're giving up the search for the fifth man,
so he would be coming round tonight.'

'Then they may well be on the murder. I can imagine his language
if he is assigned to it. He can be quite fluent on occasions.'

Susan laughed. 'He's always been the same, ever since I can
remember. I don't know how many times Papa whacked him for
using bad language.'

'What number in Cumberland Road?'

'It doesn't give a number, only the name, Kaysome.'

I groaned. 'God! what makes people choose names like that?

Katherine's Home, or Kitty's Home, or Kenneth's Home, or whatever the K stands for. What's it say?'

'Almost nothing, just a few lines that a Mr. Alex Naughton, of Kaysome, Cumberland Road, S.W., bookmaker, was found dead when his housekeeper returned home about eleven o'clock last night after a visit to a local cinema.'

'Oh well, the evening papers will probably give the gory details. They have a weakness for anything to do with bookmakers.'

She sat down on the bed beside me. I slipped an arm about her waist. Beneath the nylon housecoat and nightdress her body felt warm and deliciously soft. She turned her head, and her eyes smiled at me.

'Did you miss us last night?'

I nodded. 'Damnably. Do you realize it's the first time since our marriage I've ever returned to an empty home?'

'So it is.' She bent over and kissed me. 'But until Robert was born you were at home all day long and almost every day without me.'

'I know, but it's different being in the house alone all day and returning at night to an empty home.'

'Poor darling! But it *was* your suggestion I should spend the day with Mother and leave the children there for the night.'

'I know, and I don't regret it. Poor old dear! She doesn't see much of you in these days.'

'That's your fault.'

'Mine! What a ruddy lie. Why, I like her—'

'Of course you do, darling.' She sealed my lips with another kiss. 'You couldn't be nicer to her.'

'That's because I'm grateful to her.'

It was her turn to look astonished. 'What for?'

'Having given birth to you, sweetheart. But for your mother I should probably be still a selfish, self-opinionated old bachelor.'

She sighed with sensuous pleasure. 'You're a nice, nice husband.'

'That doesn't stop me realizing that you haven't told me why it's my fault your mother doesn't come to see you.'

'Because you're a famous author...'

I sat up. 'You haven't told her...'

'About John Ky. Lowell? Of course not, darling. That's our own special, special secret, yours and mine. But to Mother, Iain Carter is famous, an Artist, and a Creator with capital A and C. Even a genius. All of which means that you mustn't be disturbed in any circumstances.'

'With two kids already in the house a sewing bee wouldn't be worse, still less your mother.'

'Iain Carter, how can you exaggerate so? You know they're as quiet as quiet, especially Lindy.'

I grinned at her. 'That,' I assured her, 'is the understatement of the year.

In spite of our fears that Edward would not be along in the evening, he did, in fact, turn up. Of course he looked tired, that was to be expected. If he was on the Cumberland Road case he had probably been up most of the previous night.

He slumped into his usual chair and stretched his long legs their full length.

I made a move towards the cocktail cabinet. 'The usual?'

'Please.' He sighed with anticipation. 'Be a pal and make it a double.'

'Then you are on the Cumberland Road case?'

'Yep.'

'We wondered whether you might be. Waller with you?'

'Yep—except that you might say I'm with Waller.'

He finished half his glass in one gulp, then breathed heavily. 'I needed that. Didn't get more than four hours' sleep last night.'

'Then you don't want to talk?'

He grinned wearily. 'And see you going crazy with impatience! I'm more physically weary than mentally. The latter will come in about two hours' time from now.' He finished the rest of his whisky. I refilled his glass, though normally he rests at two tots.

'Know anything about Alex Naughton?' he asked.

'Only what's in the morning papers: that he's a bookmaker, and was found dead by his housekeeper when she returned home from the cinema. Do they live alone in the house?'

He shook his head. 'Not normally. She has a teen-age daughter living with her, but she had gone away for the week to visit her father in a Newcastle hospital, after he was involved in a truck smash.' He rightly interpreted my expression. 'The parents were separated about four years ago, since when he moved up north and Mrs. Rowntree has worked to keep herself. About eighteen months ago, when this man Naughton moved into this neighbourhood from Bloomsbury, he advertised for a housekeeper. Mrs. Rowntree answered the advert., and was taken on. She and the daughter, Phyllis, moved in and have been there ever since. Apparently the arrangement made everyone happy.'

Edward paused to offer a cigarette and light one for himself. As he leaned back, preparatory to resuming his account of Naughton's murder, I reflected, not for the first time, what a good-looking man he was. No wonder Anne had fallen in love with him. Although he was essentially masculine, his intensely black hair and small toothbrush moustache, his brown weather-tanned complexion, his dark-brown eyes, and his Italian-style clothes made him look vaguely exotic, an impression which had more than once blinded criminals to the width of his shoulders. Men who had been encouraged to tangle with him had found out for themselves that he made a dangerous opponent. Not only was he immensely strong, but he was quick, and knew more about all-in wrestling and judo than many professionals. At boxing he had been police champion three times.

'You know from the newspapers that Naughton was a bookie. A very successful one, too, if his home and his clothes are any indication. The kitchen alone had enough gadgetry to make Anne weep with envy; Susan, too, come to that. Same with the bathroom, same with the sitting-room. Remote-control TV, stereo-radio, L.P. gramophone, cocktail cabinet, pile carpet, easy chairs, the lot. He had a wine cellar that would have tempted you to bump him off for its contents.

'He had an office in the High Street where he did most of his business. But according to Mrs. R. he was ready to do business wherever he was, and that included his own home. He had several clients who preferred to settle their accounts with him there rather than the office, so callers were by no means uncommon.

'That's the background. Now for last night. After giving him the evening meal Mrs. R. went off to the Odeon, Naughton having said he wasn't going out. She got back from there something after eleven. The exact time doesn't matter much, for death took place, according to Doc. Pickering, between about seven-fifteen and eight o'clock.'

'What time did Mrs. Rowntree leave the house?'

'Seven-twenty, as a matter of fact.'

'At which time he was still alive?'

'Yes. He was going upstairs as she went out of the front door.'

'Why the front door? Isn't there a back door?'

He chuckled. 'You're the smart one. Any time I'm ill you can sub. for me. I'm sure you'd love working with Waller, the bastard! But it's a good question, and I put it to Mrs. R. The answer is simple. In her own way she's a snob, and refused to use the tradesmen's entrance. And I know what you're thinking. If anyone was keeping the place under observation he knew Naughton was now alone in the house, if he knew that Phyllis R. had gone north, if you follow me.'

I answered his chuckle with a grin. 'In other words, the crime was premeditated?'

'Was it? There are these points to consider. First, that Phyllis only made up her mind to go north to her father last Sunday, and didn't leave the house until the following morning. Only someone having a reasonably intimate knowledge of the household would have known that Phyllis wouldn't be at home.

'Second point. Mrs. R. didn't make up her mind to be out for the evening until just after five-thirty. As a matter of fact it was Naughton who suggested her going to the cinema.'

There was a note in his voice that warned me what he was thinking. 'You think he might have been expecting a visitor?'

He nodded. 'It's a possibility. At any rate, expected or not, there are no signs of the visitor's having broken into the house. It looks as if he let the man in—assuming it was a man—on his own...'

'Any suggestion to the contrary?'

'No, but I've told you often enough how essential it is for a detective to keep an open mind about anything and everything, until the evidence against any one person is a hundred-per-cent positive. As I was saying, we think he let the man in and took him to the back room which Naughton used as a sort of study-cum-office. There the visitor murdered Naughton, and coolly let himself out of the house.'

'How? I mean, how did he kill Naughton?'

'Strangled him.'

'Was there a struggle?'

'No, there wasn't. Naughton was sitting in his chair, behind his desk, almost as though he had leaned back to think out a really witty reply to an amusing question.'

'Amusing! Poor devil, he can't have found it amusing.'

Edward made an impatient gesture. 'Don't take me literally, for God's sake.'

'But why no struggle, Edward? And how did the visitor strangle him? Wasn't the desk in the way?'

'He was strangled from behind, with a tourniquet. He didn't have a chance. First the murderer coshed him with a rubber cosh, then strangled him before he could recover consciousness. At least, that's Waller's theory.'

'Not yours?'

'Mine as well, except that I am not convinced he was coshed first.'

'What about medical evidence?'

'Still waiting confirmation.'

'Why do you doubt the coshing?'

He moved uneasily. 'Everything apparently went too smoothly for my liking. As we see it, this is what happened. About seven-thirty Naughton is sitting in the front room, watching television—we know that because the set was still switched on when we arrived at the house—there was a standard light switched on—and by the cigarette in the ash-tray which he had only just lit when the front-door bell went. He stubbed it out, went to the door, let in the visitor, and showed him into the back room.

'There was a chair in front of the desk, an arm-chair. Did the visitor sit in it? We can't say. There was an ash-tray on the desk, close to the visitor's chair, but no match, ash, or cigarette stub, so he didn't smoke. On the other hand, Naughton did. He sat on his chair, drew it up to the desk, then lit a cigarette which he had nearly smoked when he was killed: most of the ash was in a tray on the desk: the rest of it on the floor, the stub falling from his mouth on to his lap, then on to the carpet at the moment of his being killed.'

'Lucky it didn't set fire to the carpet.'

'It wasn't luck. The murderer put it out by stepping on it.'

'You mean, deliberately?'

'Yes. It was just under the desk. He could have reached it with his toe, by stretching out his foot, under Naughton's leg, but he couldn't have stood upon it.'

'A cool customer.'

'Too bloody cool, for my money, Iain. But to go back. Naughton was sitting at his desk; the visitor, in my opinion, still standing. I think there must have been a few moments of conversation—I'm allowing for time taken to smoke nearly three-quarters of a cigarette. Then what we think happened was this. The visitor took a wad of notes from his pocket, walked up to the desk and placed it on the desk before Naughton. While he was counting the money the visitor killed him.'

'Just like that!'

'Yes, just like that. Having killed his man he then picked up his money again, all but five pounds, and left the house.'

I frowned. 'How the hell do you know the murderer brought a wad of notes with him?'

Edward raised his dark, foreign-looking eyebrows. 'I'm surprised at you, Iain. How long would it take Naughton to count five pound notes? Not long enough to give the murderer his chance of surprising him.'

'I suppose so.'

'There was only one thing that could have stopped Naughton diving for the revolver he kept in his desk at the first sign of anything suspicious—his interest in money. Besides, there was something else on the desk, a rubber band. Ten to one it was round the wad of notes which the murderer brought with him.'

'Why did he leave five behind? As a blind to the amount he really had brought?'

Edward nodded. 'He's not only a cool customer, that man; he's crafty with it. A dangerous combination. He calculated that we should probably arrive at the truth, that Naughton was killed by a punter who couldn't afford to pay his losses, so he left five behind to try and make us think he's a poor man.'

'A poor man would have taken the five as well.'

'Ah! but that's where the murderer made his first mistake, as they all do. He reckoned we should deduce that he was too panic-stricken by what he had done to think about taking the money back. We might have done, at that, except for the rubber band and the argument that Naughton could have checked five pounds without having to bend forward and concentrate. My theory is, there wasn't a penny less than a hundred pounds in that bundle, probably more.'

'Phew! I shouldn't like to lose a hundred—' I paused, abruptly. 'That theory might be a clue.'

'Well?'

'Naughton must keep—must have kept books, mustn't he?'

'He must have, and he did, and they're being examined by a man from the Fraud Squad who's used to going through books. If we find someone who owes a large sum to Naughton he'll be asked to account for his movements between seven and eight o'clock last night. In fact, we'll check up on everybody who owes him any money at all.'

'Your work will be cut out if he was that much of a successful bookie.'

He grimaced. 'Don't rub it in.'

'Any other clues?'

'Not as yet.'

'Any fingerprints?'

'Some, but we shall be ruddy lucky if we find any that don't belong to Naughton himself, Mrs. R., or Phyllis. Ever since you blasted scribblers have exposed the methods of us 'tecs every bloody crook with intelligence takes care not to leave any. And one thing is certain, the man that killed Naughton is no fool.'

'I take it none of the people living in the road that backs on to Cumberland Road saw anything?'

'Devon Road. We're making enquiries, but we haven't any hopes. He never worried much about drawing the front-room curtains, but he was a ruddy sight more particular about the study curtains. They were always tightly drawn. Didn't want any Nosy Parkers to see what went on, I'd say.'

At that moment Susan came in, and began to talk about children. Edward had a boy, Arnold. Anne had seen to that very early on in their marriage. Three children for her, she had said. I hadn't ventured to ask her whether she had changed her mind since saying so.

6

As a writer of detective stories, naturally I was interested in the murder of Alex Naughton and turned to the newspapers as they arrived. Unfortunately, from my point of view, they seemed singularly disinterested in the crime. There was, I presumed, nothing about the murder to make it sensational. In short, it lacked sex. No woman was directly involved, nor the vaguest suggestion that, somewhere along the line, one was connected with it. I considered that the newspapers gave the murder no more space than it deserved.

As I found out, the next time Edward visited us, my judgment was a little unfair to the nationals. As he dropped into his favourite chair I noticed that he was more harassed than tired.

'How go things?' I asked.

'Bloody,' was his brief reply.

'Waller?'

He nodded. 'Is being his usual bastard self.'

I knew then that the case was going badly. During the course of the past few years I had learned from Edward quite a lot about Superintendent Stanley Waller. Although efficient at his job, he had one of those characters which cannot face up graciously to defeat. Normally good-natured and tolerant about most aspects of life, as soon as his reputation as a detective was involved, he became a hectoring, bullying, and intolerant slave-driver. If there was anything to be said in his favour it was the fact that he drove himself as much as, if not more than, his subordinates. Sleep appeared to mean nothing to him; and food, still less. A cat-nap now and again, taken anywhere; on a draughty station, in a cold waiting-room, once in a stable, sufficed to keep him going for another twelve hours or so. The same with food. A cup of weak tea and a railway buffet sandwich was a meal in itself, with the added advantage that it could quickly be consumed. Why hanker for a juicy steak and fried onions?

Unfortunately for Edward, since his promotion as sergeant, as often as not he was Waller's personal assistant, particularly on a homicide case. Wherever Waller went, there went Edward. Thus he, more than anyone else in the Force, was forced to bear the brunt of the superintendent's displeasure when things went wrong.

'There's damn' little in the papers about the Naughton murder,' I said, trying to speak casually and not rub salt in the wound of Edward's exasperation.

'With bloody good reason.' He had a free tongue, had Edward, possibly because he was more extrovert than introvert. 'There's damn all to tell.'

'No clues?'

'Not yet, but it's the past that's so blank. From the moment he settled down in this neighbourhood his life is more or less an open book, but as yet we haven't managed to go back one day beyond the fourth of June some eighteen months ago.'

'The fourth of June!'

'The day he purchased the house in Cumberland Road.'

'But surely that in itself—' I stopped abruptly.

Under uplifted, dark, not altogether unsaturnine eyebrows, he glanced sideways at me.

'Well?'

'Nothing; something stupid.'

'Let's have it.'

'No, Edward. I was about to teach my grandmother how to suck eggs.'

His tired face relaxed in a smile. 'Nothing unusual in you artistic types. You're all conceited at heart even if you don't realize that fact and act modest-like.'

That was nonsense, of course, but I did not want to start an argument. 'I suppose so.'

His grin became more pronounced. Damn him! He knew exactly what was going on in my thoughts. He said only this, however: 'Mind if I smoke a pipe?' He knew very well that nobody objected, so without waiting for an answer he began to fill it.

'You were going to say—that the house should be a clue in itself?'

'Yes. If it's his own.'

'It is, and we have made enquiries from the late owner's solicitors and house agents. They weren't able to help. All the agent knew was that Naughton, having seen the place advertised, walked into his office, asked to view, and having viewed, paid the asking price without haggling.'

'Didn't he given an address, for exchange of contracts and so on?'

'Yes, the Kenilworth Hotel in Bloomsbury.'

'Didn't they know where he had come from?'

'Apparently not. At any rate, they had no records.'

'What about the solicitors who acted for him?'

'He asked the vendor's solicitors to act for him.'

'Oh! I suppose he gave the Kenilworth Hotel as address to them, too.'

'Yes.'

'What about his bankers? Had they any records which bank he used?' I paused. 'Suppose not. Why should they?'

'You suppose rightly, old boy. Also, as you say, why should they? In any case, he didn't pay by cheque. He slapped the money down on their desk in fivers and ones, mostly fivers.'

'Good God! About six thousand pounds in cash?'

'Six thousand four hundred and ninety odd, including their charges.'

'They were a bit surprised, weren't they?'

'More than, but money's money, and as it was really none of their business...' He shrugged.

'No wonder you can't go back beyond the fourth of June. Fishy, isn't it, paying in cash?'

'Suppose so, but not necessarily so.' This was the true detective speaking, always chary to accept any fact not proven beyond all reasonable doubt.

'He must have an account now?'

'Of course, but it doesn't help. He went into the local Midland, asked to see the manager, said he was a bookie, was moving into the neighbourhood, was going to set up as a commission agent and turf accountant, and would like to open Private and Ordinary accounts. With that he pushed over one thousand for the Private and two thousand for the Ordinary.'

'In cash?'

'In cash.'

'So he must have had close on ten thousand pounds in cash when he first booked in at the Kenilworth.'

'Looks like it.'

'For my money—or for his, in this instance!—he must have been a crook. An honest man would have had a banking account; or if not, travellers' cheques for that amount. Do you think he could have been involved in one of the currency hold-ups? What about that quarter-of-a-million-pound mail-van robbery of several years back?'

'Your guess is as good as mine, Iain. We checked him up in Records, of course: prints, description, the lot, but he's clean.'

'You'd have thought the solicitors who sold the house to him could have tipped the wink to the police that he was carrying all that cash about with him, so wasn't he worth investigating?'

He shook his head. 'There you are unfair to the solicitors. After all, there are a handful of people left in this country, especially solicitors, who prefer cash to cheques when dealing with property. Besides, apart from payment in cash, everything else was normal and above-board. Lastly, the money was mostly in fivers, as I've told you; which lessens suspicion of crooked dealings, stolen money, and so on. They are more easily traced. Mail-bag robberies usually are concerned with one-pound notes, sometimes on their way to being pulped.'

'So, that's that. What about clues?'

Edward's mouth tightened. 'Nothing to speak of. All fingerprints are accounted for. The murderer must have worn gloves.'

'What about the tourniquet?'

'Home-made, of strong cord knotted and looped at the ends with a metal bar slipped through to tighten the cord.'

'Is that, in itself, a clue? The use of a tourniquet, I mean.'

'In what way?'

'It's an unusual method of killing. Sounds un-English. Don't the Spaniards go in for strangling—garrotting, don't they call it?'

He nodded. 'We've given a thought to that, but it doesn't help. Records gave us two names connected with strangling, and five men with Spanish blood, but they're all clean.'

'And the tourniquet itself?'

'Hopeless. You could buy the cord in any ironmonger's shop from here to Land's End. The metal bar ditto. It's a half-inch chisel.'

'Used or unused?'

'You mean, if it had been used one might take a leaf from the Lindberg kidnapping investigation and compare groove marks. We might, at that, but it's never been used.'

'It's a bee!'

'And how!'

'Nothing else?'

'No, blast it! How there can be I don't see. This is a case of a man coming out of the blue, ringing at Naughton's bell, being let into a house empty of anyone except Naughton himself, going straight into the back room, throwing some money on to the desk, and strangling the bookie while he leans forward counting, then letting himself out of the house again, into the blue.'

'Nobody saw him entering or leaving, or hanging about?'

'We had half a dozen men questioning every household in both Cumberland and Devon Roads. Not a ruddy sausage.'

'What about your examination of the books? Did you find names of people owing money to him?'

'Seven in all, including two women, though not for large amounts. Everyone proved an alibi, though one of the women's is not all that hot. We are keeping her in mind, but I don't think there is anything to it.'

Susan came in. 'Supper's ready.' She sniffed. 'Edward, your pipe get's more foul every time you smoke it. Isn't it time you bought a new one—or shall we give you one for your birthday?'

He snorted. 'Don't be daft, sister. It's just getting smokeable.'

'I thought Edward was looking tired tonight,' Susan remarked.

We were in bed. At least, I was, stretched out on my back. Susan was at the dressing-table, treating her face to a cleansing lotion, and other mysterious unguents; a regular nightly fifteen-minute chore. Heigh-ho! I suppose even a lovely woman can't always remain lovely without taking some care of her complexion and her figure. I'm glad I'm not a woman.

'Waller's being his usual bloody self,' I told her.

'So things aren't going well?'

'No. They haven't a smell.'

She threw a used Scottie into the w.p.b. and pulled out a clean one—she spends a small fortune on those and Kleenexes, and cotton-wool balls.

'Poor Edward! He works so hard. I wonder when he'll get his next promotion.'

'Shouldn't be too long.'

'Especially if they arrest the man who killed Naughton, I shouldn't wonder.'

'Yes.'

I saw her reflection in the mirror grimace at me. 'Tired?'

'Did I sound tired?'

'That or bored.'

'Edward was right. You are daft.'

'You men, how you stick together against a poor woman, even your own wife and sister. Anyway, I'm not so daft as not to know that that tone of voice spelled either tiredness or something.'

'I am a little tired. What do you expect, after a day's work?' I went on in a loud voice.

'Yes, genius,' she murmured in a meek voice.

'For that irony come here and have your bottom smacked.'

'Yes, sir,' she said. She stood up, removed her housecoat and exposed a lovely vision of slim limbs, and a body (in spite of having had two children) encased in a sheer nightdress. Invariably neat and tidy, she folded the housecoat and placed it on the back of a chair, ready for the morning. Then she came over to my side of the bed. 'Move over.'

I groaned, and moved over. 'Why I ever started this caper of warming your side of the bed and chilling myself to the bone twice a night, I don't know. One of these nights you'll find yourself in bed with a brass monkey.'

She laughed. 'Not you—thank heaven.' She slipped into the warmed sheets and sighed ecstatically.

'Why don't you do what other women do, and have an electric blanket or a hot-water bottle?' I asked.

'There's no need to as long as I have you, my darling. Anyway, if you insist!' She bent over and gave me a long kiss. 'There, isn't it worth being nice?'

To that there was only one answer.

Presently: 'Isn't it almost time for you to pay another visit to Jack?'

Jack was a synonym for Monsieur Paul Peugeot. I had created Jack after enjoying my tenth visit to Oscar Wilde's *Importance of Being Earnest*. I had to. I didn't want Edward to begin wondering why it was necessary to pay short visits on my own to Paris every six months or so. Trouble with a detective, he's always a detective, on and off duty. Minor incidents, which mean nothing to the average man and therefore are instantly forgotten, are catalogued and filed for possible future reference in the memory of a good policeman.

I was probably being unnecessarily cautious. We did not see Edward so very often, sometimes only once a week, but Anne very often trotted round of a morning, walking her baby. Being the natural gossiper she is, I was quite sure that anything Anne learned from us she would pass on to Edward that same evening. I can see her buttonholing him before he had properly divested himself of his overcoat. 'Edward, what do you think? Iain's gone to Europe *again*, without taking Susan. *Why* does he want to go on his own, and what *does* he do there?' Not because she has any personal feelings about what I do or don't do, she's a good scout, but Anne is Miss Curiosity herself. And Edward would wonder *Why*, and *What*.

So I played golf with 'Jack' every now and again, and even Anne scarcely gave a second thought to my going with him beyond saying, on one occasion: 'Why does anyone want to play golf with *you*, Iain? You're such a bad player.' Trust a sister to rub that fact in.

'Well, isn't it?' demanded Susan, with a thump to remind me that I hadn't answered her. 'What were you thinking about?'

'Of that waitress in the Bar Anglais,' I murmured absently. 'Name of—'

'Beast!' she hissed, taking her revenge.

I caught an early 'plane, and reached Paris in plenty of time to visit the bank before going on to do some innocuous shopping for Susan.

The clerk recognized me. 'Good morning, Mr. Phillips. We've been expecting you. Your usual credit arrived from London nearly two weeks ago.'

I nodded. 'Couldn't get here sooner. I was delayed at Cannes.'

'A very nice place to be delayed in at this time of the year.' There was a vague envy in his voice. 'Is it warm down there?'

He did not catch me out. Before leaving London I had taken care to check up on the weather in the Riviera.

'Warm but rainy. It scarcely stopped all day last Wednesday.'

'That cheered him up. 'It was sunny in Paris,' he said triumphantly. 'If you will excuse me.'

He went away to consult records. When he returned: 'Six thousand five hundred and fifty new francs—and a letter.'

'Tell me in old francs. It sounds more impressive.'

He grinned. He was a friendly chap who had joined the Paris staff from a Kensington branch. 'Six hundred and fifty-five thousand francs.' The figures rolled off his tongue.

'That's better. Makes me feel like a millionaire.'

'In currency, as usual?'

'Please.'

If he was curious to know why I always collected the money in currency his face did not reveal the fact. Probably he and the rest of the staff had given up wondering why, and took me to be an eccentric playboy son of a rich industrialist who preferred Europe to his native country.

After I had paid the money into Deekes Wendell's account at the Crédit Lyonnais, I telephoned Monsieur Peugeot to tell him I was sending him a cheque for 6,300 francs on account of syndication sales of Iain Carter books, and a copy of sales report, original having been forwarded direct to Mr. Carter.

He thanked me in extravagant language—with good reason, for no man ever earned 315 francs more easily—and asked me whether I would care to dine with him that night. I was glad to be able to tell him the truth: that I was catching a 'plane abroad that afternoon.

He sounded genuinely sorry. I think he was curious to meet the mysterious American, to persuade him, no doubt, to handle other of Monsieur Peugeot's authors.

'Next time then, monsieur?'

'If it can be arranged,' I promised, most insincerely.

Then lunch at my favourite restaurant. While I sipped an aperitif I opened the letter which had been sent to me c/o the bank. As I anticipated, it was from Wen, to enclose royalty statements and to inform me that, as usual, he had remitted the money to Paris. He finished up by drawing my attention to the enclosed letter. This I had not noticed until then, it having slipped down to the bottom of his envelope. The enclosed envelope, addressed to John Ky. Lowell, Es., c/o the publishers, was buff-coloured, and marked O.H.M.S.

This, I reflected morosely, is going to spoil my lunch.

It did.

Inside the envelope was a printed memo., asking whether I had made an income-tax return for the current year, and if not, requiring me to do so immediately. Failing to do so, it seemed, would involve me in dire penalties...

7

'But you've nothing to worry about,' said Susan when I showed her the letter. 'You've declared every penny you've received from John Ky. Lowell royalties, and paid tax on it.'

'My conscience is easy, it's not that I'm worrying about,' I gloomily explained. 'It was deducted by Wen's, and a return made, in the name of Roger Phillips. The point is, how am I to let the Inspector know I've already paid tax without revealing that John Ky. Lowell and Iain Carter are one and the same person?'

'Oh!' A momentary silence. 'Oh dear!' she continued.

'I'm a damn' fool,' I burst out. 'I ought to have anticipated this.'

'Why?'

'There's a note printed at the bottom of every royalty statement to the effect that publishers are required to make a return to H.M. Inspector of Taxes of all payments made in respect of Copyrights and Royalties, and that details of such will be submitted in their official return in respect of the author's earnings. Having made a return of the money it didn't occur to me that the tax wallahs wouldn't realize this, and check up.'

'You mean, some horrible inspector has spotted the fact that x pounds have been paid to John Ky. Lowell, but that no tax has apparently been paid in respect of same.'

'Not quite. He knows that tax has been paid. I think it is surtax he's worrying about, and if he doesn't soon receive an explanation he'll put their own blasted version of the C.I.D. on my tracks. From what I've heard of them they're worse than police detectives. They're like ruddy bulldogs. Once they've sunk their teeth into a man they never let go until he's either paid up or gone to jail. Nor do they leave him in peace thereafter. They go through all his subsequent returns with a tooth-comb.'

'But you've paid.' She added, anxiously: 'You can prove you have, darling?'

'Easily. At least, my accountant can, but to do so we've got to make the Inspector a party to the secret of Lowell's real identity.'

'Aren't all income-tax matters strictly confidential?'

'Yes, but...'

'But what?'

'It means I must let Jones into the secret as well.' Jones was my accountant.

'You can trust him. He won't say a word.'

'He'd better not. He's doing well out of me for the time being.' I scowled. 'I thought I had built an impregnable wall of secrecy round Lowell, and now this. Damn all H.M. Inspectors of Taxes.'

'Hear, hear!' Susan echoed with feeling.

'Be a dear, Iain, and see the children into bed. They're all washed and everything. Make sure that Lindy says her prayers. Just lately she's been trying to forget.'

'Will do. But what's the rush?'

'You like your cheese soufflé just right, don't you?'

'Ask a silly question! How long?'

'Ten minutes.' She vanished down the stairs.

I saw the children into bed; enjoying every moment of their impish, tantalizing pranks. I had never cared for babies and young children before Susan presented me with two of my own. For that matter, I still could not stick other people's. But one's own children are different. Sometimes it mystified me. Fatherhood was beyond my simple, uninhibited comprehension. Why should one's own children mean so much to a man? Motherhood I could appreciate. After so much discomfort, pain, and even danger on occasions—that, and the knowledge that the child had come out of one's own body, made it part of one, as it were. But fatherhood was different, his share in creation being almost fortuitous. It would have been more comprehensible to me if fathers turned against their own children, for coming between him and their mother, for attracting so much of her care and attention from his needs and comfort, for ageing and disfiguring her before her time. But no. Most fathers, I had found (and certainly I was one of them), adored their children not much less fiercely than did their mothers.

As usual when I was with them I lost count of time.

'Iain.'

Susan sounded impatient, so I gave Lindy a final, hurried kiss and ran downstairs.

'I'm sure you spoil them,' she grumbled, shooing me into the dining-room. 'If you had your way I think you'd keep them up till midnight.' She vanished into the kitchen, reappeared with the soufflé. As she set it down on the table she glanced expectantly at me. 'How is that?' There was a note of triumph in her voice.

'The best ever,' I told her with sincerity. It was a magnificent effort and, in the event, tasted as good as it looked.

We enjoyed the meal, but there was nothing unusual in that: we enjoyed most meals we were able to have on our own. Our years of marriage, and two children, had not lessened our love for each other. On the contrary. We had grown still closer, I think.

We had scarcely finished eating when Edward and Anne arrived.

'Oh dear!' said Susan, as she brought them into the dining-room, 'why didn't you 'phone or come half an hour earlier? Iain and I have made pigs of ourselves with a cheese soufflé. There would have been enough for all four of us. Sit down and let me make you one.'

'We're not staying, Susan dear. We're on our way back to our own supper, with my mum and dad.' This from Anne.

'So that's how you come to be out at this time of night! They're baby-sitting, I suppose.'

Anne nodded. 'I wanted to buy a new dress from Maybelle, so Edward called for me on his way home. As we were passing here...' She paused.

Edward snorted. 'She hasn't the guts to tell you the truth. What I said was that I'd give my left hand for a cup of coffee, a real strong one.'

'He's so tired,' Anne added with a solicitous glance at her husband.

'I'll make some for us all,' said Susan. 'Coming to keep me company, Anne? The men can go on into the sitting-room and roast their toes before the fire.'

'Men *are* lucky,' grumbled Anne as she followed Susan out. 'Always being waited on hand and foot. If I could wave a wand I...' Her voice faded into the kitchen.

'Waited on, my foot!' I laughed. 'I'd be washing the dishes this very moment if you hadn't dropped in. Coming?'

We made ourselves comfortable before the fire. I saw Edward slowly unwinding, and kept silent to hasten the process. Presently he pulled out his pipe and tobacco-pouch, and was soon puffing clouds of blue smoke into the air.

'Now I won't want to go in a hurry,' he muttered.

'A drink?'

'No, thanks, old man.'

I knew from his manner that he would give anything for one, so I ignored his polite protests and produced a selection of bottles. 'Brandy?'

'Don't forget, we haven't eaten. Gin-and-French, please. But you have a brandy.'

As I finished pouring out the drinks our wives returned with the coffee. As Edward and I had hogged the only two really warm spots in the room we had to rearrange ourselves, and I had to pour out more drinks. At last we were all comfortably settled.

There was a short silence, broken eventually by Susan. 'Tell him, Edward, or he'll burst with impatience and I shall become a widow for the second time.'

'Tell him what?'

'As if you don't know! Sometimes, Edward, you can be so annoying I can't think how Anne came to marry you.'

'Hear, hear!' Anne confirmed.

Edward grinned, but I noticed that it was a very weary, reluctant grin. 'If you mean the Naughton case—' He shrugged. 'Still damnall. We're up against a blank wall. I don't remember so clueless a case since the Putney Heath murder.'

'Which was never solved, officially.'

'Nor unofficially. But if there are no clues there are one or two elements in the case that are not one-hundred-percent straightforward.'

'For instance?'

'You remember my telling you that our financial experts were going through his books. They found entries of a handful of people who owed Naughton money. I also told you they were all able to prove good alibis with one exception: one of the women's alibis was not as watertight as we wanted. We investigated further, and were able to prove one for her which she knew nothing about, so she's clean, too.

'The point is this. While they were about it the experts checked on the state of his finances as a whole. And bloody good it was, too. In five years he's quadrupled his capital—and lived well in the meantime, with his housekeeper, his Jaguar, his expensive furniture, his office staff, and all the rest of it.

'But one curious fact has come to light. Analysed out, his "bearer" or "cash" cheques, presumably for domestic and personal expenses, don't add up to five hundred a year.'

Anne looked puzzled. 'Should they add up to more than that for just one man and a housekeeper? You don't spend as much as that on food, and there are three of us.'

'I said domestic and personal expenses, Anne,' Edward patiently explained. 'We don't eat out at the most expensive restaurants two or three nights a week—'

'I wish we did. It would be gorgeous not to have to cook a meal every night and wash up afterwards.'

'Maybe, but it would cost a minimum of twelve to fifteen pounds a week per person, which means the best part of seven hundred and fifty pounds per annum in my arithmetic.'

'I still don't understand...'

It was my turn to speak. 'She was always bottom of the class for intelligence, Edward. Look, Anne, in words of one syllable, if you draw a cheque for ten pounds each week for all domestic and personal expenses, how can you afford to spend fifteen pounds a week dining out three nights a week? What about meals for the rest of the week, the housekeeper's wages and National Health Insurance stamp, cigarette money, and all the other oddments which cost money?'

'Oh! Now I understand.' She looked so pleased with herself that we all laughed. One can't help loving Anne in spite of her accent.

'What do you make of it, Edward? Has he been fiddling the income tax; has his accountant been cooking the books—?'

'Wouldn't you think he would be more likely to falsify his expenses upwards not downwards?'

I could see he was keeping something back. 'Give,' I urged.

'It's obvious that he's been paying most of his expenses in cash which doesn't appear in his books, either in or out. Waller's idea is that his income for the past year was larger than revealed by his books, and that he concealed the fact by paying in cash rather than cheques which would have shown that his expenditure was larger than his income, a possibility that was not consistent with his increased capital.'

'I wish I could follow what they are talking about,' Anne whispered to Susan.

'It isn't easy, is it?' was Susan's diplomatic comment.

I looked at Edward, wondering what was in his mind. 'If so, it is a matter for the income-tax people, not the C.I.D. You're not suggesting his fiddling has anything to do with his murder?'

'Waller isn't.'

'But you are?'

He hesitated. 'I'll go no further than to say, possibly.'

'You think some punter has lost money to him which isn't shown in his books.'

'That—or Naughton was a blackmailer.'

Quite suddenly the newspapers realized that nothing appeared to be happening in the Naughton case. No doubt, one of the morning papers found themselves short of sensational news and told the crime reporter to get busy. Whereupon he thought out a striking headline:

THE UNDETECTIVES AT UNWORK
NAUGHTON MURDER STILL UNSOLVED

Why it happened that rival newspapers came out that same morning with similar cracks at Undetectives and the Naughton Murder is a matter for reflection. Coincidence? Could be, of course, but as I happen to know that very little goes on in an editorial office that isn't known within hours or even minutes in the offices of rival editors, I have more belief in the existence of an efficient grapevine than in mere coincidence.

The effect of this resurgence of Undetective taunting was immediate and demoralizing. Superintendent Waller developed a worse fury than any his subordinate officers had previously experienced. He first lashed them with his tongue, then harassed them with his demands for further, longer, and greater efforts. He left them in no peace. Before long the poor devils were so dog-tired they fell out among themselves. Q divisional headquarters was no place to be in, according to Anne, who had been told so by Edward in language that was satisfyingly lurid.

When it was learned that Waller was under similar pressure from the commissioner, via the assistant commissioner of their section, via Commander Simpson, there were further groans, from the detective-constables upwards. As if Waller wasn't bad enough, without his being worried from above!

A few contemplated giving in their resignation from the Force and going in for farming instead. Farming might not, would not, bring in a comparable pay packet, but, by golly! it was a flaming sight more peaceful.

We did not see Edward for several days, but one night, just when we were contemplating bed, he turned up.

'I saw the light in here and knew you hadn't gone to bed,' he explained as he sank wearily into his favourite chair. 'Can you put up with me for…' He glanced at his watch. 'Good God!' he exclaimed. 'It's already ten-thirty-five. Say until eleven?'

'As long as you like. The kids won't wake us much before five-thirty.'

'Don't take any notice of what he says.' Susan looked severely at me. 'Stay as long as you like. But why…' She paused.

'Why am I here instead of at home? I've been home, got there soon after seven. After the meal I tried to settle down to the telly, but I couldn't stick it out. I told Anne I was going for a walk, and she was to expect me when she saw me. She understood, and said she would go up to bed about now.'

'The Naughton case, I suppose.' This from me.

He shrugged. 'Indirectly. Directly, it's Waller. He's being an absolute bee. He's driving the ruddy lot of us nuts, me most of all. It's the fault of the blasted newspapers as much as anything, with their bloody undetective this and undetective that. By God! I'll tell you this, if we ever get a chance of having our own back on Mr. Bloody Lowell…'

I felt uncomfortable, and did not dare to meet Susan's glance. I'm sure it would have been reproachful. Self-reproachful, I mean, of course.

'A drink?'

'No, dammit, I can't keep on accepting your drinks all the time.'

'You look as if you could do with one.'

'God knows I can!' He lifted his head. 'Yes, I'll have one, Iain. A long, strong one. Next time I'll bring a bottle…'

'You'll do nothing of the sort,' Susan said firmly. 'Iain isn't so hard up he can't give my brother a drink when he wants one.'

So we had drinks. 'Feel like talking?' I asked him.

'As a matter of fact I do. There's something buzzing here [he touched his forehead] that I daren't mention to Waller in case he thinks I'm as crazy as he's trying to make me. If I can talk it over with someone, if I can hear myself putting it into words, and then listen to what the other person has to say, I think the whole thing may become clearer to me.'

'You're rousing my curiosity.'

He took a deep gulp of whisky and .005 per cent soda. Then he mopped his forehead, although I hadn't noticed it sweating at all.

'You know how far we've got with our investigations to date. Precisely nowhere. The killer took every conceivable precaution to make sure he's never likely to be charged with the crime. I've always believed that every criminal makes one mistake, and that's what the smart detective looks for. To change the subject for the moment. Your Crime Writers' Association! Can anyone join?'

'Depends what you mean by anyone.'

'A non-writer.'

'You wanting to join?'

'Not ruddy likely.'

'Then what's behind the question?'

'Suppose you answer first.'

'I had a reason for asking. We have two classes of membership. Full and associate. I don't know which you want to know about. To be a full member the applicant must have published at least one crime book, fiction or non-fiction, or have had a crime play produced, broadcast, or televised, or have had a number of crime short stories published.'

'To be an associate?'

'To have an indirect connection with publication or production of crime stories or plays. A publisher, a reviewer, a producer, and so on. But we might make a C.I.D. man an honorary member, I shouldn't be surprised.'

Edward grunted. 'Wait until you are asked. What about fans?'

'Not on your life. We'd hate to be pestered by fans.' Susan giggled. Even Edward, in spite of his solemnity, grinned. 'I'll believe you, thousands wouldn't. Then Naughton, for instance, wouldn't have had any hope of qualifying for membership.'

'Naughton! Are you serious?'

He prevaricated. 'Would he?'

'Not unless he's written something along the lines I've listed. Why do you want to know?'

'Just that he wrote to the secretary and applied for membership, that's all.'

'Good God!'

'We found a letter from the secretary in his desk. It was dated nearly two months ago. She regretted having to inform him that he didn't qualify.'

There was something about Edward's expression that worried me. 'You don't think the letter has anything to do with the murder?'

He shrugged. 'Your guess is as good as mine. You know the old story of what makes a detective tick, especially that bit about five per cent intuition. It's that five per cent that's turning me into a fit subject for the nut-house. Without any good reason to support my theory, still less a real clue of any sort, I believe I know who killed Alex Naughton.'

'Edward!' Susan's voice rose. 'That's wonderful. If you're right, what a wonderful chance for you to win promotion. Oh dear! You've made me excited.' As he had, indeed, for her face was flushed below shining eyes. 'Who is it?'

He gulped. 'You won't really think I'm off my nut or something?'

'Of course not. Why should we? Who is he?'

He looked at me, a little nervously, I thought. Afraid I should tear his theory to shreds.

'John Ky. Lowell,' he muttered.

8

I heard Susan gasp with indignation and was afraid that she might be indiscreet. I spoke quickly, to forestall her.

'With who else as accomplices?' I jeered. 'The Director of Public Prosecutions and the Earl Marshal?'

Edward looked disconcerted. 'I'm not joking.'

'Of course you are,' Susan said sharply. 'Of all the ridiculous nonsense!'

He glanced at her with puzzled enquiry. 'Why?'

'Well, isn't it?'

'I shouldn't have made the suggestion if I thought it nonsense, Susan.'

'You don't mean you are really serious?'

'I know it's a long shot, and may sound nonsensical, but can you tell me of any reason why it couldn't have been John Ky. Lowell?'

Behind Edward's casual manner I detected an unhealthy curiosity at Susan's surprising attack on him, but before I could get a word in Susan spoke again—in her normal, even manner this time, from which I knew that she, too, had sensed her brother's reaction.

'Of course not, Edward dear. It's just the normal human inability to believe that anyone in the public eye can possibly be guilty of a horrible crime. Have you found some clue or other which made you suspect him?'

I hoped that Edward was not aware of the hint of mischief in her voice: now that she was recovering from her surprise she was obviously realizing how ridiculous and yet amusing his suggestion was. I could almost hear her thoughts: Poor dear! He must be slipping.

'Not really,' he confessed. 'In fact, no.'

'No clue!' She was so astonished she raised her eyebrows, something I have never noticed her do before. 'Then why suspect Lowell out of the fifty-or sixty-odd million people who live in the United Kingdom?'

Susan's words jogged my intuition. 'Edward, old man, you're not trying to tell us you suspect Lowell merely because you, and the rest of the police, have a hate on for him?'

He winced. 'I hope not. I don't think so, but—well, I'll tell you about that later. To answer your question first. Don't think I picked Lowell's name out of a hat because we can't think of anyone else who might have murdered Naughton. I didn't. There's reasoning behind my vague suspicions. Even Waller sees that.'

'You told him! What did he say?' Knowing the superintendent, I imagined he had a lot to say.

Edward grinned. 'Before or after?'

'Before or after what?'

'My explanation.'

'I can imagine what he said before. Afterwards.'

'He's given me the green light. "By God!" he said, "I'd give my right eye to pin it on that bastard. Find him and bring him in for questioning. Just bring him into this building, that's all I ask. Just bring him in, and I'll teach him a few things that even he doesn't know about the police."'

'And you said there was no hate on!'

He uncrossed and recrossed his long legs, another sign that he was not feeling too happy. 'Of course there's a hate on. What do you think, after what he's done to the police with his bloody Undetective. But Waller's a detective first; and a pretty good one at that, even if I do loathe his guts as a boss.'

I took a long drink, and refilled the glasses. I felt in need of some Dutch courage. 'Having taken Lowell in to divisional headquarters, then what?'

'You know the drill almost as well as I, you've brought it into your books at least twice. Politely but firmly he will be asked whether he would care to account for his movements on the night in question, between the hours of seven-fifteen and eight-thirty. If he can prove a watertight alibi...' He shrugged. 'Somebody will have to think up a new name, and it won't be me.'

'And if not?' To my ears my voice sounded husky.

'We'll throw the book at him, and every man in the C.I.D., Central and all divisions alike, will help to throw it.'

'But surely you can't ask him to go to headquarters without some good reason for suspecting him?' Susan protested.

'You were going to tell us,' I added.

He nodded. 'Here goes. To begin with, there are two things in common between John Ky. Lowell and the man who murdered Naughton. A brain capable of planning a complicated and meticulously detailed crime—'

'Come off it, Edward. What's complicated about a man's going into Naughton's house to pay his gambling debts and, finding it empty of anyone else aside from the two of them, suddenly taking advantage of the moment to save his money by killing the bookmaker?'

'That's not bright for you, Iain. Finding the house empty of anybody but the two of them wasn't fortuitous. The murderer knew it was going to be empty and, in my opinion, saw to it that it was.'

'How?'

'By telling Naughton he wouldn't go in unless it was empty. The crime was premeditated from first to last.'

'What makes you think so?'

'The instrument used by the killer, to begin with. Nobody goes about with a do-it-yourself tourniquet in his pocket. Nor does he take care not to leave fingerprints about unless he has reason for not wanting them to be found. Do you remember my theory that he had taken a large number of notes to Naughton?'

'Yes.'

'And that he had deliberately left five pounds behind to make us believe that a small punter was the killer, and had left the money behind in his panic to be out of the place?'

I nodded. 'The rubber band destroyed that reasoning. Wouldn't a man, with the meticulous attention to detail you are trying to make Lowell out to be, have taken care not to leave the rubber band behind?'

'Ah! You are forgetting the one mistake that sooner or later most criminals make. I think leaving that band was the murderer's. Anyway, don't you agree that the false clue, if it was one, was blasted clever, the type Lowell likes to work into his stories?'

'Yes,' I agreed with reluctance, in the belief that it would be foolish to try and argue against the apparently obvious. He mustn't think I had any good reason for wanting to dissuade him from thinking Lowell guilty of the crime.

'Then there was the tourniquet. That, too, smacks of the type of intelligence that Lowell undoubtedly has.'

'In what way?'

'Why did the murderer strangle Naughton with a tourniquet rather than kill him by a more conventional method? To make us poor bloody undetectives think he was a foreigner, possibly a Spaniard. My bet is, he's nothing of the sort; and if he isn't, then he's obviously the opposite: in short, an Englishman.'

I stole a glance at Susan. She was looking more tense than mischievous. I took another pull at my drink before commenting on Edward's last words.

'Damned if your imagination isn't as twisted as Lowell's.'

He took this badly, and scowled slightly. I hurriedly continued: 'Anything more?'

I thought by his sulky expression that he was going to shut up like a clam, but after a moment's reflection he relaxed.

'We've wondered why Lowell has gone to such lengths to conceal his real identity, haven't we?'

'Well?'

'Suppose he's someone who mustn't in any circumstances be connected with Lowell's books, such as a high-ranking police officer! Which brings us back to the C.W.A.'

'If you say so! I'm damned if I see how.'

'Suppose Naughton arrived at the same conclusion, that Lowell has a more powerful motive for keeping his identity secret than anyone suspects.'

'Suppose,' I echoed.

'Isn't it possible that Naughton tried to join the C.W.A. in the hope of discovering Lowell's identity?'

'Well?'

'You're slow for once,' he commented with impatience. 'In words of one syllable, to blackmail him to keep it quiet.'

'But he didn't find it out.'

'How do you know he didn't?'

I gestured vaguely. 'He wasn't admitted a member of the C.W.A., was he?'

Edward snorted. 'There are more ways than one of killing a cat. If you ask me he found out by some other method. That's why Lowell killed him.'

Going to bed that night was much less happy an affair than normally. Neither of us spoke much, not even while Susan was giving her face its beauty treatment. Not until she slid into bed beside me did she begin to speak of the thing that was worrying her.

With one arm curled up under her neck, and the other round mine, she stared up at the ceiling.

'You don't think Edward is slipping, do you?'

'Good lord, no! What makes you think he might be?'

'This nonsensical idea of his, that John Ky. Lowell could be the murderer. If it had been your theory, I mean, if you weren't Lowell, I'd understand. You are a man of imagination: it's your work to think out such fantastic theories, but Edward...' She was silent for a time.

'All his life,' she presently continued, 'Edward has been excessively realistic; too—too—too unimaginative, though I hate to use one of those horrible *un* words, in the sense that he has never allowed imagination to sidetrack him. I think it's that particular quality which has made him such a good detective. And now this. This absurd, ridiculous, fantastic theory. Just because Naughton wanted to join the C.W.A.'

'There's sound reasoning behind it, darling.'

'Not really. He might just as well have picked on any one of a dozen thriller authors who write under two different names.'

'You're wrong there. Those other people haven't gone to such lengths in covering up their trail. In fact, some of them are making a point of publicizing a pseudonym, especially if one name sells much better than the other.'

Another long silence. 'Iain, dear...'

'Well?'

'Suppose the police find out who Lowell is, there's certain to be a lot of publicity, isn't there?'

I grimaced. 'You can say that again.'

'Will it do any harm?'

'To Edward it may.'

'To you, I mean. I suppose it would be reported in every national newspaper that Iain Carter was John Ky. Lowell.'

'*The Times* might ignore the fact, the rest probably wouldn't. But if you are asking would it affect my sales, I don't know. Most publicity is good for sales, but, on the other hand, once the identity of Lowell is no longer a mystery, it's possible that his sales might drop.'

'Why should they? Your books are good enough to be read for themselves, not just as a by-product of cheap publicity.'

Dear Susan, in her loyalty so indignant at the idea that anyone should not want to read my books.

'You know what the public are like in these days of TV publicity. They're only interested in the product they saw on the telly last night. What they saw advertised the week before last couldn't mean less to them.' If I was bitter there was good reason for my feelings on the subject. I am more interested in proved quality than in publicized claims for miraculous performances that are normally disproved only in the columns of *Which*.

'The public are a lot of sheep,' she angrily exclaimed. 'But suppose the police find out that you are John Ky. Lowell?'

'You heard what Edward said. They'll ask me to prove an alibi for seven-fifteen to eight-thirty.'

'Is that all?'

'As far as I know.'

'Then you've nothing to worry about. It might not even get into the newspapers.'

'It's not quite that simple, darling.'

'Why not? Once you've proved your alibi that's that as far as Lowell is concerned.'

'Yes, once! The trouble is, I don't think I'll be able to.'

'Don't be ridiculous. Of course you will be able to. For one thing, I shall be able to vouch for you. Who else do they want, in heaven's name?'

'You can't vouch for me. That's the night you went to your mother's. You didn't get back here until after nine.'

'Iain! It wasn't that night!' She sat up. 'Wasn't it the first Thursday of the month?'

'Yes.'

'Didn't you go to the C.W.A.?'

'Yes, and a dozen members saw me there. The trouble is, I left just about seven, and I was home before half past.'

'Then?'

'I lit the fire, turned on the radio, helped myself to a whisky and a cigarette. I was there when you got back just after nine. In between times nobody saw me, therefore nobody can prove where I was.'

'Did anyone call during that time?' Her voice was sharp with anxiety.

'No.'

'Or ring up?'

'No.'

'Then you can't prove any sort of an alibi whatever?'

'No.'

'Oh my God!'

'Hey, Susan, there's no need to get het up—yet! Just because a man can't prove an alibi that isn't to say he's a blasted murderer.'

'I know that, darling. Just as *I* know that you of all people couldn't murder anyone, especially a man you didn't know existed. But what will the public think? You know how mud sticks.'

'The public be blowed! It's the ruddy police we might have to worry about!'

'No, Iain, not the police. They would soon find out you're not guilty...'

'If they tried hard enough.'

'Of course they would try.'

'Are you sure they would be all that anxious to prove John Ky. Lowell innocent?' It must have sounded as though, in a matter of seconds, Susan and I had reversed roles, that it was I who was being pessimistic. But I was still pretty confident. 'Let's not cross our bridges till we come to them. The C.I.D. are not going to find it too easy to catch up with me.'

'Are you sure? Iain darling, I'm beginning to be worried. I know Edward. Once he gets his teeth into anything he won't let go, especially if he's encouraged, to hold on. By the sound of things the police are so mad with you he will be. What do you think their first move will be?'

'They'll send somebody, Edward probably, to Cassins to ask for the address of John Ky. Lowell. That won't do them any good. Cassins will tell them they don't know, and refer them to A. B. Wen.'

'Mr. Wen wouldn't give the Press any information at all.'

'I know, but keeping mum where the Press is concerned is one thing. I doubt whether he'd care to obstruct the police. I rather think he'll tell them everything he knows, which, thank God! isn't much. All the information he can pass on is that he has always written to me care of either Cooks or the Westminster Bank in Paris. That and the fact that my real name is apparently Roger Phillips.'

'Then what? Will they send a man to Paris?'

'I don't know. It might not be necessary to do that. They may visit the head office in London of both concerns, and initiate enquiries from here. It won't help them much, and even if they do send somebody over, it won't add anything. The Westminster people could only report having paid the money over to a Mr. Roger Phillips, on instructions from England, and after that, nothing. Absolutely nothing. I can promise you that.'

'Couldn't the bank clerks over there describe you?'

'Up to a point, yes, but will that help? To begin with, I've always worn a hat—'

'But you never wear a hat.'

'Exactly, that's why I've always taken that old black felt of mine to Paris. Also, I've worn slightly tinted spectacles, a French tie, which I wouldn't be seen dead in over here, and that check suit that makes me look like something out of the Hippodrome chorus of the early twenties.'

Beginning to relax, she laughed. 'You really do have a tortuous kind of brain, don't you, darling?'

'A relic of Boy Scout days. Be Prepared and all that.'

'What about the French bank?'

'The Crédit Lyonnais. They know me as Deekes Wendell.'

'Dressed as Roger Phillips?'

'Well, yes, but there's absolutely no reason whatever to connect Phillips with Wendell. If the C.I.D. ever follow up as far as Paris they'll probably imagine that, as I always draw cash, I spend it in riotous living somewhere on the South Bank, or in Montmartre not a hundred metres from the Place Pigalle. I could, too, quite easily. If you knew what it costs to have a night out in Paris.'

'Instead of which you bring it all back to spend on a dull, extravagant wife and a couple of demanding children.'

'Dull be damned!' I told her, pulling her towards me.

We heard nothing more from Edward for several days. We heard of him, from Anne. What we heard was not reassuring. After two days of intense activity, on the morning of the third he flew to Paris.

After hearing that, life lost something of its savour for both Susan and me. We were silent for most of the time. When we did speak, our conversation was particularly flat and uninteresting. It was not that we were anxious, at least I wasn't, but the strain of waiting for more definite news unsettled us.

But life goes on. So does business. On the fifth day, after Edward had metaphorically thrown a bomb at us, I had lunch at Kettners with an editor who was dithering with the idea of commissioning Iain Carter to write half a dozen articles on crime. It was a pleasant meal, and the general gaiety of the diners made a welcome change from the gloomy atmosphere of the past few days. To add to the pleasure of the day, I was duly commissioned for the articles at fifty guineas per article. Feeling that I ought to pay for the lunch I pleaded to have that privilege, but the editor was a sport.

'Next time,' he said.

My mood of jubilation disappeared as soon as I saw Susan's face.

'What is it, darling? One of the children...?'

She shook her head. 'It's Edward. He rang to make sure you would be in tonight.'

'Why?'

'He and Superintendent Waller want to see you. Oh, Iain—Iain—I'm so afraid...' She crept into my arms and buried her worried face in my shoulder.

9

The next few hours were hellish. I can't say how many times I glanced at the electric clock, but not once had it advanced as much as fifteen minutes. I did not try to do original writing, but took up some galley proofs of my next Iain Carter book. When I found I had read one galley without having consciously absorbed a word I gave that up, too, and tried to read. No good, I was too fidgety.

I had not found it easy to calm Susan. She should have known better, of course. Having lived much of her life with a policeman she should have had more faith in justice; have realized that the chances of an innocent man's being found guilty are a million to one against. She should have understood that the mere fact of my not being able to prove an alibi would not, of itself, tell against me in the absence of other evidence. But her love for me, bless her, prejudiced her against police investigation, and would not allow her to regard my possible danger with dispassionate judgment. I think she saw me already in the dock.

At last the afternoon merged into evening. The clock crept slowly on to the hour of 8 p.m., at which time the two C.I.D. men were due. Having picked with gloomy disrelish at a hasty supper, and put the children to bed, we sat in the sitting-room, waiting. I had set out the coffee table, with coffee cups, glasses, and bottles ready, in the hope they would take drinks, but I wondered whether they would. One does not normally take drinks with a man one suspects of murder.

I switched on the radio, but all three wave-bands sounded equally dreary. I tried commercial TV instead, but when one of those terrible singing advertisements began, Susan protested.

'Please turn it off, Iain. I don't think I can stand any more.'

I was happy to oblige. To think civilized people have to put up with such drivel as the price for viewing a programme of doubtful merit. I returned to my chair, and stared into the fire.

'I can't think why they should want to speak to you, unless...' She stopped abruptly, and flashed an apologetic glance in my direction.

I replied with a sickly grin. 'Unless they've found some evidence against me?'

'Yes, but...' She shook her head. 'How could they find evidence against you if you haven't committed the crime?'

I shrugged. 'God knows! And as we, too, ought to know, at any moment, it's not worth worrying ourselves round the bend.'

My words were a signal for the door bell to ring. Susan gulped as she rose hurriedly to let them in.

I'll say this, there was nothing alarming about the expressions of our visitors. On the contrary, Waller seemed as cheerful as his normally gloomy face allowed him to look.

'Hope we're not butting in on anything, Mr. Carter,' he began. 'If so, you must blame your brother-in-law. It was he who persuaded me you wouldn't mind us dropping in like this.'

Wouldn't mind! I saw Susan's face, behind the backs of the two men, begin to glow with relief. She laughed, and if the sound of her trill had a touch of forced gaiety about it, I was the only one apparently to be aware of it.

'I should have blamed him if he hadn't brought you. Let me take your things.'

'We mustn't stay,' the Super hastily protested. 'I assured your wife we shouldn't keep you more than a few minutes.'

'You must stay long enough to have a drink.'

Waller glanced doubtfully at Edward, who nodded his head. 'Iain's idea of a friendly evening is to send his visitors home half seas over, sir. He'll raise hell next time I come if I don't persuade you to stay.'

'I don't need all that persuasion.' The Super began to strip off his overcoat.

'You hang up the coats, Edward, while Iain gets the drinks,' Susan ordered.

The Super was quick enough to settle in the most comfortable chair in the room—mine! When Edward returned he gave me a tired wink.

'To be frank, Mr. Carter,' Waller began, 'I am grateful for an opportunity to relax for a time. I suppose you've heard from your brother-in-law what a hell of a time we've been having with the Naughton case.'

'Not directly. He never tells me a thing about the cases he's working on until the people concerned have been put inside.' May I be forgiven that lie! But I didn't put it above Superintendent Waller to try and trap me into betraying Edward, even though he was about to accept my drink. Never misses a trick, does the superintendent.

'*When* we put them inside,' he commented sourly. 'We don't seem to be getting far in the Naughton case.'

''Course, I've had suspicions things weren't going well.'

'Why?' he demanded sharply.

'We've seen so little of Edward since it broke. On the odd occasions I've seen him he looked so tired and glum I've put two and two together.'

'And made the correct answer of four.' The Super's voice was a little sour, I thought. Apparently he realized he was being reproved in the nicest possible way.

'Well, what about those drinks?' I looked at Waller. 'I think I can offer most everything.'

Before he could answer, Edward spoke. 'Excuse me, sir. Are you making coffee, Sis?'

'Can't you smell it?' Susan moved towards the door.

'I thought I could. In that case, sir, if you feel like a brandy, ask him for one. He can afford to keep it in hand, not being a ruddy policeman.'

'Anyone can afford to *keep* it,' I assured Edward.

Waller chuckled. 'Sergeant Meredith knows my weakness.' He nodded. 'I am tempted.'

I poured out the drinks. Edward asked after the children, pointedly stressing the fact that he hadn't seen anything of them for God knows when, which made Waller look sour once more. Susan came in with the coffee. The four of us settled round the blazing fire.

Waller supped his cognac appreciatively. 'I suppose you're wondering what this invasion is about, Mr. Carter.'

'I thought it was for the pleasure of our company.'

Edward looked angrily at me; a warning that I shouldn't allow my tongue to get too sharp. Evidently I was not supposed to accept Waller's affability at its face value.

'Well,' Waller began awkwardly, 'while I am enjoying myself...' he glanced first at the brandy then at the fire, 'I have to admit that we have a purpose in calling on you, Mr. Carter. In short, we should appreciate your help.'

'My help!' I was genuinely startled.

'I understand from your brother-in-law that you are a member of an association of crime writers.'

'The C.W.A.?' I nodded.

'You meet once a month?'

'On the first Thursday.'

'Next Thursday. Would you take us there as your guests?'

'Of course! The members will be delighted. Any policeman is manna to us.' I looked enquiringly at him. 'Are you proposing to write a book, Superintendent?'

'God forbid!' He paused. 'Mr. and Mrs. Carter, forgive me, but if I reveal something of our investigation in the Naughton murder, may I have your word it will go no farther?'

'Of course.'

Susan nodded.

'Well, then…' Again he paused, this time with embarrassment I thought. 'There are reasons to believe that Naughton was killed by a writer. A crime writer.'

'Good God!' I tried to look startled. 'One of our members?'

'Ah! We do not know.'

'Tell me his name. I have a list of members in the study.'

'I doubt whether his name is on it. I am speaking of John Ky. Lowell.

'Lowell! Well, I'm damned!'

Waller raised a warning hand. 'We can't be sure.'

'Lowell!' I repeated, as though I thought the idea too preposterous for serious consideration. I shook my head. 'If he is a member I wouldn't know. Nor would anyone else for that matter.'

'Are you sure?'

'If you knew the number of hours we've already spent arguing! I should be very surprised to find out that Lowell is a member. We should have pried the fact from him by now.'

Waller looked disappointed. I glanced at Edward. He was looking mulish, and nobody can be more mulish than he, believe me.

'We'd still like to go with you, if it's all the same, Iain,' he said.

'Gladly. Will you meet me there, any time after five-thirty?'

Waller nodded. 'Thank you, Mr. Carter. We shall be there. You must realize,' he went on, pompously, 'we are skilled at interrogation. It is our business. A moment's hesitation, a twitch of a nerve, all kinds of mannerisms can tell us a complete story. If there's anything to be learned we are more likely than your members to find it out.'

'I realize that,' I assured him with humility. 'All the same, it's hard to believe that John Ky. Lowell could be the murderer.'

'Why?' Waller baldly demanded.

'I don't know why. Because I'm a crime writer myself, I suppose. Besides, there seems no apparent reason for the crime. Why should a crime writer want to kill a bookie, unless he owed the chap a hell of a lot of money?'

'According to Naughton's books nobody owed him any money of consequence. Certainly not enough to make anyone commit murder to avoid paying. As for other motives...' Waller's manner turned condescending. 'Motives are not always obvious. For instance, is there any reason why the two men, the murderer and the murdered, might not have fallen for the same woman? Jealousy may have been the cause of the killing. Or don't crime writers indulge in extra-marital pleasures?'

I conceded that trick, and gave him a sickly grin. 'So that is what Lowell has been up to?'

'I didn't say so,' the Super sharply contradicted. 'There is nothing to suggest that he has. I quoted that as an example only, as far removed as possible from the real facts.'

'You mean you really have evidence against him, and aren't pursuing him from malice?'

The Super winced, and looked uncomfortable. 'We certainly are not pursuing him, Mr. Carter,' he said with the brusqueness of a guilty conscience. 'That is a most unfortunate word to use in speaking of our investigations. We have a clue which points to his guilt. A few words with him will quickly tell me whether he is innocent or otherwise.'

'You mean, if he can prove an alibi, then that's that.'

'Precisely.'

'And if not?'

Waller shrugged. 'If he can't prove an alibi I think he will find it hard to convince us he's not the man we're looking for.'

*

They stayed awhile, chatting lightly on topics other than the Naughton murder. As soon as they had gone Susan's brave front collapsed. She flung herself into my arms.

'Iain darling, I'm frightened. Suppose they find out who John Ky. Lowell is.'

'Don't worry, they won't.'

'You don't know Edward, especially with Superintendent Waller to drive him on. He's like a bulldog.'

'But I do know him, my love. He couldn't very well be my brother-in-law without my getting to know something about him, could he? I still say, don't worry.'

It took time to calm down her fears. Scarcely had I done so when Edward returned.

He sank into his usual chair. 'If you've another drink to spare, Iain, old man...'

'Of course.' I poured one out, passed it over to him. 'Waller?'

He nodded. 'He must have been an overseer of slaves in one of his previous incarnations.' He took a long pull. 'Thanks for covering up about me giving you inside dope in cases.'

'I thought he might have been fishing.'

'He was doing that right enough, damn him!'

'You've certainly convinced him that Lowell was the killer. He talks as though the evidence against him is strong.'

'Strong's not the best word, but... I've not seen you for some time, have I? There's something damn' funny about the lengths Lowell goes to to conceal his identity. When Waller gave me the green light I went along to his publishers to ask for information. According to them they know no more about the man than anyone else.'

'They must know something. Where do the scripts come from, to begin with?'

'From A. B. Wen and Son, a firm of literary agents. Know anything about them?'

'By repute. Among the three best, I'd say.'

'I went to see them.'

'The newspapers didn't get anything from them.'

'The newspapers!' Edward shrugged. 'I let them know that what was good enough for the newspapers wasn't good enough for the police. They opened up.'

'They told you Lowell's real name?'

'Yes. It's Roger Phillips.'

'Roger Phillips! Where does he live?'

'Ah!' Edward looked morose. 'That's where the funny business begins. Wens don't know where he lives, nor in what country for that matter.'

'They must communicate with him at times. Where do they send his royalties, for instance?'

'Mostly to the Paris branch of the Westminster Bank. Occasionally elsewhere. I flew over to Paris to find out what happened to the money. Phillips collects it in cash.'

'The bank doesn't know where he lives?'

'Not the least idea.' Edward banged the arm of his chair. 'Lowell, or Phillips, or whatever his real name is, must be a crook. Only a crook would want to cover up his trail to that extent. And if he's a crook, no wonder he knows enough about police and crime to write so realistically.'

'I thought you suspected Lowell of being a policeman.'

'I did. At that, he could be. What's the difference between a crook knowing a hell of a lot about the police, or a policeman knowing too much about crime? And if he is a crook, and Naughton knew it, there's your motive for you.'

I did not dare to look at Susan. Instead, I glanced at her glass, and noticed that it was empty.

'Another drink, darling?'

'Please.'

Edward glanced at her. 'Cold coming on, old girl?'

'I don't think so. Why?'

'Your voice sounds husky.'

'Just a frog.' She made a to-do of clearing her throat.

I filled up all three glasses. Susan wasn't the only one who needed another drink.

'So Lowell conceals his address, acts mysteriously in money matters, and knows more than most about police and crime. But surely you're not all wasting so much time on mere supposition?'

'No, Iain, we're not,' he agreed. He stopped absent-mindedly to fill his pipe. 'There's this. During a final visit, two days ago, I came across it, tucked inside a book in Naughton's sitting-room.' He took something from his wallet and passed it over to me to look at.

It was a clipping from the advertisement columns of the *New Daily*, announcing the forthcoming publication of a new John Ky. Lowell book.

Edward stayed another fifteen minutes or so, but nothing new emerged. Perhaps because I did not press him for any more information. I was too nervous about the possible effect on Susan. I could see that she was as tense as it was safe for her to be, particularly so considering how steady her nerves and composure normally were. I hoped Edward wasn't similarly conscious of her unusual condition.

No sooner had the front door closed upon him than she was in my arms again.

'Iain, oh, Iain—' she began.

'Not now, dearest,' I said firmly. 'We're going straight up to bed. By the time we're ready for bed you will have had an opportunity to realize how absurd it is for anyone to get into a panic.'

'But, darling—'

'Not until we're in bed.'

So we went upstairs. It was the earliest we had gone up to bed for many months—since Susan's last pregnancy, in fact.

10

S usan sat before her mirror, brushing her lovely hair. By then
I was in bed.

'Are you sure nobody called?'

Her voice was calmer, I noticed. My Susan was her old self again;
composed, reflective. Although we had not exchanged a word for
fifteen minutes or so I knew what the question meant.

'Afraid not.'

'Did anyone see you come in?'

'Philip Rankin might have done. He was closing the curtains
and waved to me as I passed. But whether he did or not makes no
difference. The fact that I entered the house doesn't mean I didn't
leave it again.'

She sighed. 'If only I had 'phoned. I nearly did.'

'Why?'

'Can't tell you why. Just wanted to hear your voice.'

'Surely you hear it enough?'

'I suppose so. Silly, isn't it, but all the time you are away from
me I'm counting the minutes to your return. I couldn't have enjoyed
the day with Mum and Dad more, yet I was impatient to be leaving
the moment the clock struck seven, when I knew you would soon
be due home.'

She didn't have to describe her feelings to me. I was the same
where she was concerned. Any time I was in Paris alone I wasn't able
to enjoy the place as much as I ought to, just because she wasn't with

me to share my pleasure. On two occasions I had caught an earlier 'plane than planned, just to be with her that much sooner.

Another long silence. Having finished with brushing her hair she began to cream her face.

'Iain...' she said at last.

'Susan.'

'Suppose, just suppose, the police find out that you are Lowell, and you aren't able to prove an alibi, surely that silly scrap of newspaper isn't enough for them to charge you, is it?'

'I shouldn't have thought so, but it's not the risk of being charged I'm worried about, but the ensuing publicity. I can just see the bloody newspapers. "Mr. Iain Carter, a writer of crime novels under that name, and the author of the more famous books by John Ky. Lowell, has been at the headquarters of the Q division since one o'clock this afternoon. It is reported that the police hope that Mr. Carter will be able to assist them in their enquiries into the death of Alec Naughton, the bookmaker." Damn them!' I raged as I saw Susan shiver. 'Even if nothing more happens, some people will wag their silly heads and say "You can't have smoke without fire."'

'Don't, Iain, please.'

'Sorry, darling. Must be on edge myself.'

'Is that surprising?' she whispered. She wiped traces of cream from her face. 'I wonder why Naughton took the trouble to cut that advertisement out of the paper.'

'Perhaps he likes—liked detective stories. I've seen you clip adverts of books.'

She nodded. 'Just for once I wish your Lowell books were not so popular. If only he had cut out an advertisement for one of Edward Grierson's books, or Maurice Proctor's. Or even Iain Carter's. Anybody else's but Lowell's.'

I wholeheartedly agreed. I couldn't think why Naughton should have been so interested in John Ky. Lowell, unless...

Susan must have been watching the reflection in her mirror. 'You've thought of something?'

'It's far-fetched, but for want of any other explanation! Given that Naughton was a blackmailer, and that he has read all the fuss in the newspapers about the mystery of Lowell's identity, the advertisement might have suggested a new victim. So he cut it out to remind himself that he might try to find out for himself who Lowell is.'

'Perhaps.' But I could see in the mirror that Susan wasn't entirely convinced.

Another silence followed. Susan finished beautifying herself and came towards the bed. I duly moved over on to the cold side. She got into bed, and, leaning on one elbow, gazed down at me. Her eyes were suspiciously moist.

'I couldn't bear it if anything were to happen to you, darling.'

'It wouldn't please me much,' I said lightly. 'Anyway, why should it? John Ky. Lowell is as innocent as an unborn child of Naughton's murder.'

'As if you have to tell *me* that.' With a sudden, passionate movement she fell back upon her pillow, and wrapping her arms about me hugged me so tightly I could scarcely breathe.

'Iain,' she said at last, 'don't you think it would be a good idea to tell Edward?'

'That I am Lowell?'

'Yes.' Perhaps she anticipated my reaction to this suggestion, for she quickly continued. 'It would bring an immediate end to police investigations into Lowell's identity.'

'Think so?'

'I do. He would know at once that the police were wasting their time.'

'Would he? Suppose he should ask me where I was at the time of the murder?'

'Nonsense! He wouldn't ask anything of the sort. His own brother-in-law twice over, and a good friend, too! He'd know you were innocent, and that would be the end of that.'

'Optimist! I don't think you know Edward as well as you think. He's a detective first, and a friend a long way behind. My betting is, he'd ask the question.'

'Suppose he does.' My doubts seemed to irritate her. 'All you need do is to tell him the truth. He will believe you.'

'Perhaps!' I wished I could feel as sure of that as Susan was. 'But you are forgetting Waller. He's sunk his teeth into the Lowell solution, and isn't likely to let go because Edward changes his ideas.'

'Then...' She paused. 'Edward could pass on the information—in confidence,' she added in a small voice that warned me she didn't have much faith in this idea herself.

'And commit employment suicide! Don't be silly, darling. If ever it should become known that Edward is Lowell's brother-in-law he'd be out of his job so ruddy quick he wouldn't even know who booted him out. D'you think they wouldn't guess who'd given me all the inside dope about police investigation?'

'I wish you had never invented Lowell,' she exclaimed passionately. Her rigid fingers dug into my flesh.

'Makes one think, doesn't it?' I agreed morosely. 'But when you remember what his royalties mean to us!'

'I suppose so. But if we pledged Edward to secrecy?'

'No,' I firmly refused. 'It wouldn't be fair to Edward, to make him muzzle his conscience. Besides, we've nothing to worry about, darling. I swear I've covered up the trail.'

I think it must have been the revelation of the depth of Susan's love for me that prevented my falling asleep that night. I knew she loved me, but the measure of her love terrified me. No man could be worth that much love. I'm sure I wasn't.

If anything should happen to me, what would it mean to her? The idea made me feel sick. She wouldn't commit suicide, or do anything weak like that. If only for the sake of the children she would face the future with resolution. But what kind of a future? It didn't bear thinking about.

I had assured her that the police would never uncover my trail, but was that claim, I wondered, too optimistic? Dispassionately, I reviewed the 'life' of John Ky. Lowell from the moment of conception. Except in connection with the Paris bank I couldn't find a loophole. The cashiers at the Westminster would be able to give a description of me—had already done so, in all probability—but I was still convinced it wouldn't be recognizable as me. Not even to Edward.

In fact, it can't have done, assuming that this had already happened. Edward would have added something to this effect: 'Lowell's about your age, I'd say, Iain. Not unlike you, if the description's anything to go by.'

No, unless Edward should find out that I had been over to Paris once every six months or so, I didn't have to worry about the past. But make a note, I told myself in parenthesis, never to let him examine my passport, even casually. The English might not stamp an English passport with a ruddy date stamp, but the French did.

SÛRETÉ NATIONALE

P. A. BEAUVAIS

6 MAI

& 7 ENTREE A

and

SÛRETÉ NATIONALE

P. A. ORLY

10 MAI

SORTIE A

7

Even though I used the Phillips passport every other trip, a number of these dotted about Iain Carter's passport would tell their own story if the dates should be compared with those of payments made by the Paris branch of Westminster Bank.

It was the future I was worried about, for I knew how long police memory is, and how unbending their patience. Knowing now that it was the custom of A. B. Wen & Son to send royalties to a European city, mostly Paris, every April and October, they would certainly keep the bank under observation, and wait for Mr. Roger Phillips, alias John Ky. Lowell, to claim the money. That would be their cue to accost me.

(Are you Mr. Roger Phillips, otherwise known as Mr. John Ky. Lowell, a novelist?

Yes.

We'd like to ask you a few questions in connection with the death of Alex Naughton, on the night of…)

No more running over to Paris to collect royalties, but what was the alternative? To have them sent to Brussels, or Amsterdam, or Dieppe, or Madrid instead? I had only to telephone Wen, to give him the name of the chosen town, but would he communicate with the police? Not willingly, I was sure, but if they'd asked [sic] him to co-operate?

The only solution of the problem I could think of was to wait until the whole damned affair had blown over for one reason or another. Of course, that would mean having to do without royalties for a time, but however inconvenient (ruddy inconvenient) that would be, it would be better than being exposed as Lowell, at the best, or being charged with murder, at the worst.

No sooner had I decided upon this course than I appreciated the danger involved in it. If I didn't claim the royalties within a week or so of their being sent, the reason for not doing so would become apparent to Waller and Edward. They would be reasonably sure that Lowell had learned of the trap.

Inevitably their suspicions, through the process of elimination, would work round to me. At first they might merely conclude that I had been too free with my tongue, and they would look upon me as a bloody gossip. But it would not take long, I believed, for two intelligent brains to begin adding two and two together. And then...

No wonder sleep eluded me.

After a minimum of sleep, the following morning I was in no mood for work. I tried, of course. If writers worked only when they felt in the right mood, many fewer books would be published—which might not be a bad idea! But worry is an effective stopper to creative work, so I gave up trying to finish Chapter Five of a John Ky. Lowell book, and gave up the rest of the day to the problem of what to do for the best.

I couldn't blind myself to the fact that I was in a subtle trap. Unless someone else was charged with murdering Alex Naughton, sooner or later I was going to have to answer some mighty awkward questions. And with the divisional C.I.D. directing much of their efforts to pinning the guilt on John Ky. Lowell, I didn't see them arresting anyone else in a hurry.

A pity they couldn't find a clue which would draw them off Lowell's scent and put them on someone else's, I reflected. That would leave me free to collect the next lot of royalties when they became due. With their attention fixed on somebody else, even if they did hate Lowell's guts, the police wouldn't care less what he got up to, as long as it was legal.

First things first. How to escape the trap I was in? It was fine to indulge in a bout of wishful thinking about clues and so on, but nothing was more unlikely than the surprising appearance of a new clue at this late date. The police were neither fools nor negligent in their duty. It was certain they would have sifted Naughton's belongings with a metaphorical tooth-comb.

*

Precisely when the first glimmerings of an idea occurred to me I cannot say. Probably because I didn't give it a second thought at the time. I was dealing with reality, I reminded myself, not drafting out a plot for one of my books.

Some time later, after I failed to evolve any way out of my difficulties, the idea returned to me. This time I considered it more conscientiously. If it really were a case of desperate measures...

A false clue! A crazy idea, and yet... But what clue? How to plant it?

Instinctively, I glanced at my over-filled bookshelves. Autographed editions of novels by members of the C.W.A. occupied two complete shelves. It wouldn't take two minutes for several among that crowd to work out means of planting a false clue in a place where the police would accidentally come across it—which meant Naughton's home (his office having already been let to someone else). They'd think out a character like Raffles, or The Saint, or The Toff, who'd find that sort of thing child's play. But me! Thanks to Edward I knew a lot about detectives and crooks, but gentlemen cracksmen weren't in my line.

Besides, what was the use of planting a false clue in Naughton's house? Edward had spoken of a final visit. The police were unlikely to go there again without reason.

Next point, what could the clue be? What would make the C.I.D. men decide that Lowell was innocent and that somebody else was probably guilty of killing Naughton? And where would one find that elusive something?

Having wrestled with this problem for a couple of hours I decided that it was a crazy idea, which only a second-class thriller writer would have dreamed up in the first case.

Crazy or no, I returned to the idea, I had to. Something had to be done. Susan's face convinced me of that.

Outwardly, she was calm. Nobody else would have realized that she was inwardly repressed to the point of doing herself harm—how many people have suffered from a thrombosis as a result of self-repression? But I knew she was sick with terror on my behalf.

'You didn't sleep well last night,' I accused, feeling guilty. I had slept like a log. A consequence of not sleeping much the night before, I suppose.

'Not too well.'

'Not too well be damned! The understatement of the year. You are worrying too much.'

'Aren't you?'

'So so. But you know how I slept last night.'

She nodded. 'I envied you.'

'Well, then, if I'm not worrying, why should you?'

'I've lived with Edward most of my life. Whatever you may think, I know him through and through. If he's convinced that Lowell might have killed Naughton, nothing will stop him worrying at the case until he's proved wrong.'

'He'll be taken off it in time.'

'Officially, perhaps, but that won't stop him. He'll keep it in the back of his mind. Unofficially, he'll watch and wait and prod and probe into every case in the division, in case it offers something, a lead, to the Naughton killing. I dare say most C.I.D. officers are the same. Waller is, for one. But there's something in Edward's character that won't allow him to be beaten. Obstinacy, pride, I don't know, but something. Are you sure, darling, absolutely sure you haven't left a clue somewhere along the line?'

I hesitated, but I had to be honest with her. 'That's quite a question. I'm happy enough in my own mind, but I can't guarantee I didn't do something I don't know anything about.'

'In Paris do you have to sign a receipt for the money?'

'Naturally, but always in a disguised handwriting.'

'Always in the right name. With all the different names you are using you might have slipped up.'

'If I had it would have been noticed at the time.'

'You always wore that awful hat, and one of those terrible ties?'

'Always. Look, darling, I really have been careful on every occasion. Edward, the Yard, Interpol, the lot, can do their damnedest. They'll never prove that Iain Carter and John Ky. Lowell are one and the same person. Apart from myself you are the only person in the world who could prove that. Why! I've even burned every page, typed or written, which has contained a single word of a Lowell story. On the other hand, there's enough Iain Carter material around to sink a battleship.'

She smiled wanly. 'I am being stupid, I suppose. If I didn't love you so much perhaps I'd be less worried.'

That's why I returned to the possibility of planting a false clue.

There's many a good story to be found in newspaper headlines, so I skim through all national morning papers, irrespective of their politics. That is how I came across a short paragraph in the *Daily Herald*, not duplicated in any other paper.

> Mr. Rex Mayer, solicitor for Cecil Reddick, who was sentenced to two years' imprisonment for his part in the recent bank robbery, is applying for special permission for the prisoner's wife to visit her husband when she reaches London on Friday. Mrs. Reddick is breaking her journey home from Australia at Marseilles so that she can fly back to England.

There must be something in the popular belief that all artists are either round the bend or a good half-way there. The truth is, I suppose, that their imaginations are highly developed. At any rate, the moment I read that paragraph something sparked off my imagination.

The idea was preposterous, fantastic, but desperate diseases are relieved by desperate cures. Refusing to heed carping common sense, I leaned back in my chair and began to examine the plan from every angle I could think of.

What were the facts? First, that, in spite of having arrested and charged four men in connection with the robbery at Barclays, the police believed that five, or even six men had been involved.

Two, that Reddick's house in Devon Road was immediately behind Naughton's house in Cumberland Road, and therefore convenient for keeping a watch on Naughton's activities.

Three, that the house had been empty for some days immediately preceding Naughton's murder, and that, according to something Edward had said, presumably nobody had entered it since members of the C.I.D. had searched it at the time of Reddick's arrest. The keys, it seemed, were in the possession of Mayer, the solicitor, pending Mrs. Reddick's return.

If there were any place where a clue could be planted, Reddick's house was a possible choice. Suppose that, on her return to London, Mrs. Reddick found evidence that somebody had been using the house since her husband's arrest, would she not immediately call in the police? Almost certainly so.

What would probably happen next? A detective would be sent round to investigate. There he would see an object that would make him connect the intruder with Naughton's murderer, and perhaps, with luck, with the bank robbers. That would be putting the cat among the pigeons with a vengeance. The probability was that Waller and Edward would hurry round to see what else was to be found there. In their search they would find a clue that would convince them of the innocence of John Ky. Lowell.

So far, so good. But it is comparatively simple for a detective-story writer to invent a novel method of murder: the difficulty lies in filling in details that will stand up to the critical analysis of the habitual detective-story reader. In short, having conceived a sketchy outline of a plan, I now had to solve far more elusive problems. To begin with, what was the object to be which would immediately make a detective associate it with Naughton's death?

I was afraid the answer to this question was likely to prove a headache, but concentrated thought eventually came up with it. A pair of field-glasses! That was the answer, sure enough. Field-glasses to suggest that somebody, Naughton's murderer presumably, had taken advantage of the empty house to make use of it as a 'hide' from which to study the victim's habits.

It did not take me long to realize that this was but half an answer. The discovery of the field-glasses would not absolve Lowell, but merely offer evidence against him by proving that the murder was premeditated.

Means must be found to tie the glasses up with a time that, if accepted by the C.I.D., would enable me to prove an alibi for myself in the unfortunate event of Lowell's real identity being discovered. The Saturday before the crime, for instance, Susan and I had gone to the England versus France rugger match at Twickenham, and afterwards on to my parents' for supper. I had an unshakable alibi from dawn Saturday to dawn Sunday.

More, concentrated thought, and soon—a solution! If you think it was all too easy, remember that it had been my work for many years to think out answers to just that kind of problem. In this instance, the answer was an evening newspaper. The Saturday night Classified Edition. Psychologically, it was good; a subtle touch. It was exactly what a criminal, of the type I was hoping to suggest, would do; take a copy of the Classified Edition to see what luck the Spurs had had, whether Arsenal had beaten the Hammers, whether Brentford had snatched a point from Torquay. That is, provided I could obtain a copy of the edition, at this late date, without drawing attention to myself.

Damn! Damn and blast! To go to a Smith's bookstall and ask for a copy of a month-old Saturday's Classified Edition would do that without a shadow of doubt. Only a crazy idiot would go to all the trouble of specifying a Saturday Classified when almost every Sunday newspaper would contain the same information, plus.

My exasperation vanished as I remembered that on the Saturday night preceding the murder I'd bought a copy of the *Evening Standard* on our way to the parents'—and I had brought it back home, in my overcoat pocket. Before going to bed I'd checked results with my Pools duplicate, and thrown the paper down with disgust. Eleven points!

I wondered what had happened to the paper. My calm detachment dissolved; I became fiendishly impatient to search through the pile of discarded newspapers which Susan keeps in the cupboard underneath the stairs until there is no room for more. Then she takes them outside into the garden, and leaves them for the dustmen. And that was today! Any moment now, in fact. I had seen her putting them out earlier on.

I was tempted to rush downstairs there and then to search through the papers before the arrival of the blasted refuse disposal squad, or, in plain English, dustmen. But that I dared not do until I had thought out a good excuse to pass on to Susan.

Do you think I could think of one? Not on your life. I fumed and fussed and stamped about, but my brain wouldn't tick over: it just doesn't like being forced. Dammit! what could I say to her? What? What? And the damned dustmen were due any second now. What? If I didn't think up something soon I'd be too late.

My sanity was saved by the sound of the front door. I rushed over to the window. Susan was below with the family, on their way to the shops.

I sighed with relief and went downstairs. Provided it hadn't been destroyed—lighting the fire, or wrapped round garbage—I might find that precious copy.

I did not find it at first rifle through. There were upward of three hundred papers. On the point of cursing life for playing such a bloody rotten trick on a man, I decided to look through again, just in case…

I found it, also the following Monday night's *Evening News*, which I abstracted from the pile. That, too, I decided to leave in the house as additional evidence—if there were any way of my breaking in, of course. But I was not yet ready to try and find a way of crossing *that* particular bridge.

As I stepped back into the kitchen with my newspapers I heard the garden gate crash open. The dustmen! Phew!

Back in my study, once more mentally relaxed, and ready to give quiet reflection to other aspects of the plan, my memory began to work. A pair of field-glasses! There was a pair in the attic; had been for the past two years. Susan had bought them in a rummage sale (£1,000 urgently needed for repairs to the Church roof. Help *your* Church. Give generously. Buy generously).

Susan had both given generously and bought generously. I had found myself short of one much-beloved suit (a little threadbare perhaps, but still usable), a hat (good riddance to that!), sundry spare copies of my own books (autographed, of course, for the sake of the extra sixpence, which experience has taught me is the precise value of my autograph), a cricket bat (a piece of nostalgic piracy, this. I had once hit a six with it), and... but why go through the list? I'm not the only husband to dread the announcement of a forthcoming rummage sale.

As for buying generously! Apart from the field-glasses (I already had two pairs, good, too, ex-W.O. surplus), I found myself saddled with an unmicroscope, an electric un-shocking-coil, an electric unrazor (110 volts only), and heaven knows what else! As Susan said at the time, looking at me lovingly with those large, melting eyes of hers: 'The Vicar did so want to make twenty-five pounds from the rummage sale. So I bought what was left at the end, all this lot for three pounds, which gave him his twenty-five, with seven shillings and eightpence over. I felt almost mean, offering so little for all those things.' So who was I to begrudge £3 towards repairing St. Mary's roof?

I went up to the attic, and turned over a trunkful of accumulated rubbish. The field-glasses were at the bottom. A tatty pair, with one lens cracked. But they were good enough for their purpose. They focussed, and would have been efficient enough for seeing into Naughton's house from an upstairs bedroom in Reddick's home. I took them downstairs and hid them. Then back to my chair for more brain-waves.

On second thoughts I told Susan of my plan. Not only do I dislike lying on principle, but I'm a bad liar—at any rate, where she is concerned. To her sharp eyes my face is an open book. The merest prevarication is detected almost before I have finished speaking.

By the time I had finished she was looking at me with horrified eyes. 'Iain! Of all the mad, insane ideas!'

'Agreed, but necessary.'

'Not that. Not housebreaking! If you were caught you would be sent to prison.'

I shook my head. 'Don't look on the worst side. If I am caught...' I paused, and added with what I hoped to be extreme confidence, '*if* I am caught, I couldn't be charged with housebreaking and/or burglary...'

'Why not?'

'The essence of housebreaking and burglary is that the person charged has entered enclosed premises with the object of committing a felony. I am sure I could persuade the court that I had absolutely no idea of stealing anything.'

'How?'

The sharp note in her voice warned me I was in for a fight. 'I should tell the court that, being a sort of amateur detective, on paper, as it were, it had occurred to me that the bank burglary and the death of Naughton might be related—'

'Why? Naughton was murdered after the arrest of the bank robbers.'

'I know, but before the robbery they had to meet some place to discuss its operation, didn't they? What more convenient place than Reddick's house? With his wife in Australia and nobody else in the house they had nothing to worry about.'

'Fair enough,' she reluctantly agreed. 'But where is the connection?'

'I am coming to that. Remember Edward's saying they were reasonably sure a fifth, even a sixth, man had a part in the robbery? It's significant that one-fifth of the proceeds have never been traced. I shall say that I wondered if the fifth man, knowing that the house would be empty until the wife's return, used it as a hide from which to case Naughton's house...'

She wrinkled her forehead. 'Case?'

'Underworld slang for keeping premises under observation with a view to breaking in. Don't you read my books, darling?'

She made an impatient gesture. 'This isn't the time for flippancy. Go on.'

'That's almost all. I should say that I was breaking into the Reddick house to see what there was to be seen of Naughton's house, to explain the field-glasses, and also to look about for any other clue to test and perhaps substantiate my theory.'

There was an awed expression on her face. 'It's fortunate for me you're a writer and not a criminal, dearest. I think you have a more tortuous mind than anyone I know.'

I grinned. 'So long as it pays dividends.'

She moistened her lips with the tip of her tongue. 'Do you really think the police would accept such a preposterous explanation?'

'It would be their job to disprove it. In other words, to make the charge stick they would have to prove my intention to steal something, which they could never do.'

'But surely people, however honest, can't just break into other people's houses without committing an offence of some kind?'

'Trespass; which, generally speaking, is grounds for civil, not criminal, proceedings.'

'You make it sound much too simple.' She spoke in a strained voice. 'Please don't go on with the idea, Iain darling. Please don't.'

'I'll not be doing it for laughs,' I assured her, and I meant that. I'm not one of your natural-born Bulldog Drummonds, or one of your Saints. 'But something has to be done before it's too late.'

'Oh God!' she exclaimed, turning her head away so that I should not see her tears.

That afternoon I went to Hampstead and bought two bottles of Watney's light ale. I went on to Putney, where I purchased a packet of cigarettes I don't normally smoke.

On my return home Susan barely allowed me time to take off my outer clothes before renewing the battle.

'How can you break into a house? You don't know the first thing about it?'

'What about *Two Shillings to Pentonville*?' This was an Iain Carter book. One of my characters in it was a burglar. I used the better part of a chapter to describe a burglary—I had recently seen a reissue of *Refifi*, which gave me the idea. I was rather proud of that chapter. Naturally, Edward had supplied the technical information.

'That!' Such a contemptuous exclamation. 'I passed a school examination on the theory of music, but I can't sing or play a note.'

This was a slight exaggeration, but I took her point.

'You're forgetting something, darling.'

'What?'

'That bunch of skeleton keys Edward gave me a year ago,' I explained.

After the evening meal I said to Susan: 'Do you want to come out necking with me?'

She looked startled, but I suppose my face gave me away. She sighed. 'Now what?'

'I want you to become an accessary before the fact. In other words, help me case the joint. You know that big cedar tree, half-way along Devon Road?'

'Yes.'

'If we do a bit of discreet necking there nobody will give us a second thought.'

'They will. They'll think we are mad, to stay out on a night like this when we could be in the back row of a warm cinema.' She nodded. 'But if you insist, I'll come with you. Mrs. Hopkins will baby-sit for an hour or so. It will be less strain than remaining home wondering what new mischief you are up to.'

'The worse the night the less people about to see us.'

She stared at me. 'Sometimes you frighten me. You have it all worked out. Shall we go now?'

'And get it over with, you mean?'

She nodded.

We walked through the streets arm-in-arm beneath an umbrella, for a drizzle was damping the atmosphere and making the pavements reflect the street lights. We both had mackintosh coat-collars turned up. With one thing and another I had little fear of being recognized. Besides, there were only a few people about. Sensible folk were enjoying their telly programmes.

Upon reaching the cedar tree we stood as close as we could to the great girth of it. I gathered her into my arms and kissed her. Her face and lips were cold, but they responded quickly enough.

'I'm beginning to think this is fun.'

'Oh, Iain! Fun!'

'Well, exciting, then. Making love all over again.'

'Thank heaven, my darling, you've never stopped doing that.'
Her arms convulsively tightened about me. 'If only—'

I stopped the rest of her words with another kiss. I really did feel
as though I had stepped back a few years. It was with genuine regret
that I buried her face in my shoulder and began to 'case the joint'.

Reddick's house was on the opposite side of the road, six along
to the left. Like the other houses in the road it was semi-detached,
two-storied, 'Tudorbethan', built, I guessed, in the thirties. The
area between each block of two houses was common to both and
concreted, leading to separate garages at the back.

The area between the two houses immediately opposite was in
dark shadow, due mostly to the fact that it was as far distant from
a street light as any in the road. On a drizzly night like the one we
were suffering one might reasonably hope to slip along it unseen
except from the two houses behind us. Unfortunately, Reddick's
house was less favourably placed, being nearer to a street light. But
the risk would have to be taken.

From where I stood I could not see how one entered the back gardens of the two houses opposite, whether through a second, smaller
door in the garage or by way of a separate door, close to the entrance
to the garage. A moment's reflection convinced me that the separate
door had to be the answer—one wouldn't expect the dustmen, for
instance, to go through the garage to collect the dustbin.

I turned my attention to the houses each side of Reddick's,
and those immediately opposite. Four or five of the houses along
the length of Devon Road had their lighted rooms open to the
passing world—a cheerful view for passers-by, and one to be com-
mended. Anything to shed a little colour and light on the gloomiest
of all scenes, an English suburban road on a dark, miserable night.
However, the rest of the houses, by far the majority, had adopted
the normal conservatism of an English family and, by drawing their
curtains, sealed themselves off from other eyes. These, I was glad to

notice, included all the houses near Reddick's. Perhaps in shame at their neighbours' disgrace, I reflected.

I felt Susan's body shaking within my arms. Poor darling Susan! I began to feel guilty; a brutish, bullying husband.

'Please don't cry, dearest. We'll go—'

'Crying!' As her body became positively convulsive I realized it was laughter that shook her, not tears.

'Susan!' I reproached her. 'If you think this is a joke!'

'A joke?' She choked with the effort to contain her laughter. 'Iain, it *is* a joke. The most superbly ridiculous joke. For a respectable happily married couple to act like teenagers, spooning under a dripping cedar tree on a perfectly atrocious night like this just for the purpose of casing a joint as you call it...' She hugged me. 'I don't think anyone else in the world would have thought out a situation like this...' Another burst of repressed laughter. I thanked heaven nobody else was within earshot. 'You must put this in one of your books,' she gasped. 'You positively must.'

'Not damn' likely.'

'But you must.'

'Don't be ridiculous, darling. In these days of realism the critics would roast me.'

'What for?'

'For unrealism.' Then I, too, appreciated the humour of the situation. I joined in her laughter.

12

'I'm going,' I told Susan the following night. 'Keep your fingers crossed for me.'

Her eyes turned bleak. 'I suppose it's no use my making one more appeal—'

'Not in the least,' I firmly assured her, sincerely hoping she wouldn't make another appeal. It wouldn't have taken much to make me change my mind about going.

'But why tonight? Why not tomorrow?'

'Tomorrow will be too late. Mrs. Reddick returns tomorrow.'

She made a gesture of hopelessness, and lifted her face for a kiss. 'If you must go, darling, at least be careful. Don't take any chances.'

'That's a promise,' I said with sincerity, before I kissed her.

Our lips clung together for many seconds, until I felt her hands pushing me away. 'Go quickly,' she whispered as I reluctantly stood back. 'While I still have courage.'

Me, too, I thought, and quickly left.

Once again I wore a hat, second-hand, bought that morning from a second-hand clothes dealer in East Ham. It was at least two sizes too large for me, and I'll say this for the dealer, he tried to persuade me not to buy it. 'I gotta smaller size, mister, jest right f'you.' But when I insisted that I liked a hat large enough to be comfortable, he shrugged, and charged me nearly twice its worth because I was a mug, and mugs is born to be gypped. I also bought from him a pair of size thirteen boots—for my brother, I told him.

Since buying the hat I had stuffed the lining-band, or what was left of it, with newspaper, to make it fit me. So at least it clung to my head, and was low enough for its limp, wide brim to shade my eyes. My mackintosh collar I wore turned up—with justification, for the night was as cold and dreary as the previous night had been.

Through practically deserted side-streets I walked a mile and a half to a fish-and-chip shop, and bought ninepennyworth of rock salmon and sixpennyworth of chips. The woman who served me barely gave me a glance; she was too busy exchanging gossip with Emily Somebody-or-other.

With this last purchase I had everything I needed. All that remained to be done, to put my plan into operation, was to gain entry into the house without being seen. Simple! So damn' simple I couldn't have felt worse going to my own execution.

I started off on the mile-and-a-half return to Devon Road. At the first opportunity I stopped to inspect the newspaper that the fish-and-chips were wrapped in. It was a copy of the *News of the World* for the previous October. Good enough. By then the newspaper was well and truly smeared with fat. I dropped the fish-and-chips down a drain, and wrapped the newspaper in a clean piece which I had in my pocket and which, with its contents, I returned there. I continued on. So did the ruddy drizzle.

Devon Road. I slackened speed as I turned into it. I might be wet outside, but my mouth was as dry as dust. I'd have given much for a drink; alcoholic for preference, but I'd have said thanks even for a fruit drink.

My feet began to drag as I neared my destination. I'd always been convinced I wasn't the stuff heroes or adventurers are made of. Now I knew for sure that I wasn't. I had to force myself onward, and this I did by reminding myself of Edward. As long as he believed that John Ky. Lowell could be guilty of Naughton's murder, I wasn't safe.

For the sake of Susan and the children I had to do my damnedest to change his ideas.

I was almost level with Reddick's house, by which time I wasn't able to breathe through my nose. As for my mouth, my tongue felt as though it had swollen to double its normal size. I stopped to light a cigarette—this is always done in detective fiction, as a means for someone to survey a neighbourhood. Fair enough. As I was able to prove for myself, it is a most effective way. To my joy there wasn't a soul about, and no window within reasonable distance was uncurtained. The moment was ideal for taking a chance on turning off on to the concrete drive-in.

Half a dozen more paces—and just as I was about to slither into the shadows, light streamed out into the street as the front door of the next-door house opened.

'So long, Bill,' said a voice. 'See you at the tennis club A.G.M.'

'Yeah. Which reminds me...'

If that wasn't to be the beginning of one of those protracted good-byes I was a Dutchman. There was only one thing to be done. Walk on.

As I always say (to the fury, I'm told, of everyone I know except dear, patient Susan, bless her), to cut a long story short, after many alarms, and several false starts, I was able, at last, to dart into the area separating Reddick's house and its left-hand neighbour. There I was reasonably concealed by its black shadows—thank heaven for a dark, cloudy night, even if it did mean putting up with the drizzle.

Pressing close to the Reddick wall I edged my way to the gate which led into the back garden. It was bolted on the inside, but I was still agile enough to climb over. Inside the garden I crept up to the back door and tried my skeleton keys in its lock. At the fifth attempt the tumblers turned. Now for it. Was it bolted as well as locked? It wasn't. The door opened to my push. Need I add that I was wearing gloves?

Having closed the door behind me and made certain that the curtains were drawn, I risked flashing my torch. I found myself in a small scullery.

Before going farther I changed from my normal shoes into the larger-sized pair I had brought with me, and which I had already made well and truly muddy. I was quite sure the C.I.D. men would find at least one of the many prints I was aiming to leave around.

I went on into another room, a small combination kitchen-dining-room.

This is where I began my work. I opened two drawers, took out knives and forks, dirtied them, dropped them carelessly in the sink. I found a half-used jar of marmalade in the cupboard, which I transferred to the table, after smearing a couple of plates with it, also butter (rancid) and some stale breadcrumbs, both of which latter I had brought with me. I also left on the table a 2 lb. bag of granulated sugar, opened and on its side, spilling out, and a candle (which I had also brought with me) which I left burning, so that it should drip grease on the American cloth which covered the table. I also made a pot of tea.

In short, by the time I was through I was satisfied that the kitchen had the appearance of having been used by an extremely untidy or careless person. Then I went upstairs to the back bedroom.

Here I tried to create the same effect. Having moved the dressing-table out of the way I brought up a small arm-chair from the down-stairs front room, which I placed in front of the window before kicking the field-glasses underneath. I screwed the fish-and-chip newspaper into a ball which I threw into a corner. I left the empty beer bottles on the dressing-table, side by side with a dirty glass (after pouring the beer into it and swallowing down some Dutch courage to sustain me!).

I flung myself down on the bed, muddy boots and all, and tossed about a bit, to leave a distinct impression of my body—*and* I took the precaution of making the impression that of a taller man than I, to agree with the size of the shoe-prints. I do not underestimate the efficiency and thoroughness of the average C.I.D. man.

I smoked a number of cigarettes I normally never smoke, and left the butt-ends in an ash-tray which I found on the bedside table. I also screwed up the empty package (I had thrown the rest of the contents away the previous night) and threw it in the fireplace (fitted with a gas-fire). The hat, minus the newspaper underneath (which I took away with me), I tossed carelessly on top of a chest of drawers. I left the Saturday Classified Edition and a Monday evening Late Final at the foot of the bed. I also burned another candle, and left used chewing-gum about.

Lastly—and, while apologizing for mentioning this detail, I must add that I do so to prove what respect I have for the C.I.D.—lastly, as I say, I made it apparently obvious that an intruder had used the toilet on several occasions. Naturally, he wouldn't have let the cistern run. No crook, however stupid or careless, would have taken the risk of letting the people next door hear the noise.

I have described these happenings in terms which might suggest that, once I had entered the house, I went about my task with unconcern. This was far from being so. I was in a state of tension every minute of my hours' stay there. Fear magnified and gave significance to every sound. Every footstep on the pavement became the measured footstep of a policeman. I didn't hear the throb of a car engine without immediately concluding it to be police on their way to arrest me. Each time the car went by not until the sound of its exhaust had completely faded was I able to convince myself I was still safe. During each period of agonizing seconds I felt sick with dread, and quite unable to move. I sweated and shivered alternately, sometimes simultaneously.

I left the house by the door I had entered, and crept along the drive-in to the road. There were no sounds to be heard, neither footsteps, cars, nor voices.

Boldly I went forward to the pavement. The road was completely deserted.

As long as I live I shall never forget Susan's response to my return. She was sitting in the same chair as when I left, and gave me the impression she had not moved from it the whole time I was away. Her face was drawn with anxiety.

She looked at me as I entered the sitting-room. Her eyes were filled with infinite love.

'Thank God!' she exclaimed in a husky whisper. She opened her arms. 'Darling, oh, darling!'

I crept into the warmth and comfort of her embrace with mixed feelings of contrition for causing her so much mental suffering, and awe to think I could be worth so much love.

About 9 p.m. the following evening the front-door bell disturbed a long period of mutual contented reverie.

Susan looked at me. 'Edward?'

'Shouldn't be surprised.'

Edward it was, looking glum and disconsolate. He sank into the arm-chair with a weary sigh.

'I'm on the scrounge again, Iain. I need a drink, badly, and can't face the idea of going into a pub. Not in the right mood, I suppose.'

'You know we're always pleased to see you, Edward, but isn't Anne waiting for you?' This from Susan, of course. Somewhat reprovingly: 'Don't you drink at home?'

'Don't be daft, Susan. You know I do. I'll have a second drink with Anne the moment I get home. I don't intend to stay long, anyway, but I thought Iain would like to hear the latest.'

'Don't take any notice of our Susan,' I told him as I passed him his drink. 'She's a feminist at heart. She always backs a woman against a man, whoever he may be.'

'Except you, darling,' she interposed.

'Sometimes you forget that I knew her first, Iain. Cheers.' He took a long drink. 'God! I needed that.'

'What's new?'

'What isn't? Everything. The whole bloody affair's gone round the bend.'

'You've identified Lowell and he's proved an alibi?'

'No.' There was a vicious, spiteful snap in his voice. 'But he's out, for the time being.'

'Out! But I thought you…' I paused.

'Go on, say it. You thought I was convinced he was the murderer. Is that it?'

'Something like that.'

'So I was. But for once it looks like intuition isn't good enough. It's all the fault of you ruddy detective-story writers.'

'Us!' If I was surprised this was because I didn't follow his reasoning.

'Yes. I've been reading too many of your books—when I've had time!' he added significantly. 'As a result, I'm falling into the habit of missing the obvious in looking for one of your damn' silly complicated solutions. Hell!' he exclaimed. 'This time I've really been led up the garden.'

'How about explaining?' I suggested.

He nodded. 'Remember the bank robbery Waller and I were working on just before Naughton got himself bumped off?'

'Weren't they sentenced a week or so back?'

'Yes. Well, you'll remember that the wife of the clerk, Reddick, was somewhere in the Australian outback when her husband was arrested. By the time she heard about what had happened it was too late for her to be back here in time for the trial.'

'Couldn't she have flown?'

'No lolly. She had to come back on a slow boat as far as Marseilles. She flew back from there this morning. She went straight off to see her husband, her solicitor having obtained special permission for her. An obliging cove by all accounts, after the interview he drove her home. Just as he was about to drive off she flew out of the house and shrieked for him to go in. Two minutes later he was 'phoning for the police to send somebody to investigate. The house was in some sort of a shambles.'

'I don't understand. I thought you and Waller were the last men to enter it after the arrest.'

'So we were, and it was tidy enough when we locked it up and delivered the keys at Mayer's office—Mayer is the solicitor.'

'Hooligans break in?'

'Hooligans be damned! No, somebody entered the place sometime after we had finished with it, and used it for spying on Naughton's home. The two rear gardens are back to back.'

'Good God!' After short reflection I looked at him with puzzled eyes. 'Couldn't whoever it was have been John Ky. Lowell?'

'I don't know.' He made a despairing gesture. 'The short answer is, Yes, he could have. But from what I've been told, I don't think so. Intuition again,' he explained with bitter emphasis.

'You've been *told*! Didn't you go?'

'No, I was down at Bournemouth all day, chasing a possible clue to Lowell's whereabouts. A blasted wasted journey. Dixon went to Reddick's house, and he 'phoned for the Super to join him. I was at the station when they returned. Dixon gave me the dope.' He frowned. 'The man who broke into the house left enough evidence behind him almost to pin-point his appearance.'

'Bit careless of him, wasn't it?' I daringly suggested.

'Careless, but not more so than the men who robbed the bank. It was their carelessness which helped us to pick them up. This other man Waller and Dixon reckon to be about six feet one inch in height, in his late thirties, with hair greying at the ears, and wearing down-at-heel boots beginning to wear under the ball of his left foot.'

'That all?'

'It's plenty to go on with.'

'It scarcely pin-points him. There must be thousands of men that description fits.'

'I said, almost,' Edward irritably corrected. 'It may be enough to help the C.R.O. to give us a lead.'

'How does the description absolve John Ky. Lowell?'

'Look, I wouldn't dare argue this with Waller, but I don't mind you. The man who broke into Reddick's house left a teaspoon in the cup he drank out of—no saucer, mark you. He lay on the bed in muddy boots. He smoked a cheap brand of cigarettes. He ate fish-and-chips out of a newspaper—all right, I can see by your face that you are thinking, so do tens of thousands of other people. But I like to believe that the majority of those people wouldn't leave the greasy newspaper about.'

'Not even in somebody else's house?'

He looked disconcerted. 'I'm not explaining myself too well, am I? This is the significance as far as I am concerned. Whoever the man is who writes the Lowell books, I am sure, from the way he writes, that he's had a good education, one of the universities as likely as not, and comes from a good middle-class background. I don't think that anyone brought up in those circumstances would lie on a bed in muddy boots, not even somebody else's bed. It's something he just couldn't do, if you follow me.'

'I follow you, Inspector Maigret.'

'All right, so I'm borrowing from Simenon. Why not? If Lowell was tired enough to lie down on the bed I'm willing to give you damn' good odds that he would have put a newspaper on the bed-cover where his boots would rest, and that he wouldn't just toss a greasy newspaper on the floor. He'd have put it in a waste-paper basket or something. Nor would he have dripped candle-grease all over the place as our man did. I'm sure, Iain, that the man who did these things in Reddick's house would have been incapable of writing Lowell's books. In short, I can see no similarity whatever in the two personalities concerned, Lowell's and the man who kept watch on Naughton.'

I was seeing Edward in a new light. Although he appeared to have accepted my false clues, his subtle reasoning alarmed me. What he said was so right. As my normal self, or as Lowell, I would have hesitated to stretch out with muddy boots on a made-up bed, or, had I done so, I should have done what Edward claimed I would do: have put a newspaper or the equivalent on the bed, to protect the cover. Although not the tidiest of mortals, I should not have left greasy newspaper about. Candles I should have stuck on a small plate or saucer.

'There's one final point,' Edward continued after a slight pause. 'If you remember, my chief reason for becoming suspicious of Lowell is his meticulous attention to detail, his ability to project himself into the mind of another man and so be in a position to anticipate that other man's reactions to any given problem. Above all, his knowledge of police criminal investigation. Well, a man with that knowledge would not have been careless enough to leave clues to his personality, still less to his physical measurements.'

'So it wasn't John Ky. Lowell, after all, who killed Naughton?'

'If the man who occupied Reddick's house was Naughton's murderer, then he wasn't Lowell,' he agreed.

But the slight emphasis with which he underlined the word *if* left me feeling a little uncomfortable.

The next news we had of Edward's progress came not from him, but from Anne, and that was two days later.

She came in for a chat with Susan. I heard her voice, but didn't go out to greet her. I was too busy. I knew she wouldn't be annoyed with me for not speaking to her. Unlike some people, she had sense enough to realize that a writer must not be interrupted at the moment of inspiration.

Just before luncheon was ready, Susan came into the study. Her eyes were very bright, I noticed, and her manner gay, carefree.

'Anne's just gone.'

I nodded. 'I heard her voice. How is she?'

'As always.' She smiled. 'I like Anne, for all her funny little ways.' She sat on the arm of my chair, and rubbed her fingers through my hair. 'She brought news. Wonderful news.'

'Already? I thought she was going to wait—'

'Not that, silly. I mean, news about you, us. Your preposterous, clever, dangerous trick's come off, darling. Edward's been taken off the Naughton case.'

'You mean, they've closed it?'

'I don't know about that. Anne didn't say. But now that Edward will no longer be after Lowell's blood, we've nothing to worry about.' She bent over and kissed me.

'There's still Waller,' I pointed out as soon as I could.

'Oh, him!' She laughed gaily. 'You don't have to worry about Waller. He's an undetective.' She caught hold of my hand. 'Coming? Lunch is ready.'

I realized that I was extraordinarily hungry.

13

After days of emotional strain, the period of tranquillity which succeeded was particularly welcome. Life settled down to a normal calm. Susan began to sing again as she went about the housework, and the sound was sweet music in my ears. The children romped and played and quarrelled and screamed, and the sound was anathema in my ears. I settled down once more to work routine.

On the Sunday, Edward and Anne came in to have supper with us. As usual, Edward's parents were sitting in—by gentlemen's agreement my parents sat in for us, Edward's parents for him. An excellent arrangement all round, which I commend to all young married couples.

Edward looked better than I had seen him for many weeks. The strain and tenseness had vanished; he looked rested.

As always in winter, we started off the evening by sitting round the fire, talking and drinking. By mutual consent, no goggle-box was permitted when we forgathered on such occasions. No anti-social, damned uncomfortable supper-trays balanced precariously on laps for us. We preferred to act like civilized human beings, even if this was so only one night in so many.

For quite twenty minutes nobody mentioned a word about crime or police or authors or books. The two women talked children. Edward and I discussed sport in general, squash-racquets in particular.

Then: 'Before I forget, Iain. Your C.W.A. meeting next Thursday. The Super said thanks for the invitation, but not to expect us after all.'

I raised my eyebrows in query.

His grin was vaguely sour. 'I'm off the case, so I'd have no excuse…'

'That doesn't make you unwelcome.'

'I know that, but another time.' He pursed his lips. 'It might be wiser.'

'And Waller?'

He shrugged. 'No, he's no longer interested in Lowell.'

'That's definite then?' I asked.

'Absolutely. He's convinced that the man who broke into Reddick's house killed Naughton.'

'But why? Where's the connection between Naughton and the bank robbery?'

'According to Dixon, Waller has three theories. To begin with, that there is no connection between the two crimes. He thinks it is possible that the killer read about Reddick being in jail, and the wife in Australia, and took advantage of the house being empty to use it for casing Naughton's house.'

I nodded. 'Reasonable enough, I suppose.'

'I think so. The second theory Waller has thought out is this, that Naughton organized the robbery and the money he was counting out when he was killed was his share.'

This suggestion startled me. I believed I had thought out every angle, but this one was new to me. One up to Waller. Or was it?

'What do you think?'

'Ingenious, but! If Naughton had a record, or even if he was known to mix with the wrong company, then I'd say he has something. But it was no amateur who organized the robbery.'

'I thought you told me they were careless.'

He raised his eyebrows. 'That's right, so I did, and so they were.' He reflected, then shook his head. 'The plan and organization smacked of the professional, but the execution was amateurish.

Humph! Super might have something there, after all, though I'd give it the lowest rating in order of priority.'

'And the third theory?'

'That there was a fifth man in the robbery after all, and that Naughton was blackmailing him.'

'What's your personal opinion?'

'I think the third is the most likely. If it weren't for the tidiness of Naughton's murder I'd go for it all the way.'

'Sorry to be off the case?'

He took time to reply. 'Yes and no. Yes, because life's easier for not being directly concerned with the case, and because I'll not have to share the rap with the Super if it isn't solved. No, because…' his lips tightened, 'I don't like admitting defeat.'

It was selfish of me, but at that moment I felt more than ever glad that he had been taken off the case. I hoped he wasn't working on it in his spare time. Had he remained convinced that Lowell was the murderer I think he would have, to prove his original theory correct, but it seemed that his ideas had been shaken by the discovery in Reddick's house. I thanked the gods for the inspiration which had suggested that plan. But for that—but that was an unsettling reflection, and I sheered away from it.

'Waller making any progress?'

The question produced a mystified expression on Edward's face. 'I don't know. He's keeping so quiet, I'd say he wasn't, but for…' He paused.

'But for what?'

'That's the point. I don't know. It's that bloody intuition of mine. I feel that something funny is going on.'

'Such as?'

'I can't tell you. I don't mean I won't. I mean I damn' well can't.'

This was Edward in a mood that was new to me. It made me wonder what was happening.

*

Tuesday afternoon Jim Newberry rang me up. An old friend of mine, he is chief constable of one of the Home Counties Police Force, one of the youngest chief constables in the country.

'How about a foursome tomorrow, Iain?'

'Have a heart, Jim. I'm one of the workers of this world, in case you've forgotten.'

'A worker!' he scoffed. 'You call yourself a ruddy worker! You don't know the meaning of the word.'

This was Jim's favourite joke, so I accepted it with what patience I could. 'I mean it, Jim. I'm behind schedule. Been interrupted quite often, lately.'

'Going to the C.W.A. meeting on Thursday?'

I wondered what made him so interested in the meeting. Were all the police in the country suddenly becoming interested in the activities of crime writers?

'Yes; why?'

'I thought you said you were busy. If you can go to that!'

That's typically Jim. A damn' good chief constable, I've been told, but where humour is concerned… Still, I like him.

'I can do a day's work before going there,' I pointed out.

He laughed. 'I know. Just my joke. But seriously, couldn't you manage tomorrow? I've been let down at the last moment. Besides, I think you would enjoy the company. Just up your street.'

'Writers! I see enough of 'em, Jim, thanks all the same. One can have too much of a good thing.'

'Not writers; 'tecs. Well, sort of. One's a big noise at Central, the other's in the D.P.P.'s office. You might learn something.'

What he said made a difference. As long as there was a chance to learn something! 'Where are you playing?'

'Beaconsfield.'

'Okay, I'll come—but it's not to be taken as a precedent.'

'All right, it's not a precedent. You can work yourself into an early grave as far as I'm concerned—after tomorrow. We're staying in Town for a few days, so I'll call for you. About eight-thirty?'

'I'll be ready.'

Being a punctual man I was ready on time. Jim was pretty good, too. Only seven minutes late.

Susan kissed me good-bye. 'Have a nice day, darling. Play well.'

Jim stared at us. 'Lucky swine!' he exclaimed.

In spite of knowing him so many years, I bit. 'Why lucky?'

'Having a wife who gives you a nice good-bye, and wishes you well. My wife just says: "I hope you slice every ball out of bounds." She thinks no man should be allowed off the matrimonial leash, unless she plans to take a friend to a matinée or what would you.'

'What a liar you are,' Susan told Jim sweetly, as she gave me a push towards the door.

It was an ideal day for golf; brisk and sunny. I think we all four of us must have been inspired. We played like champions, with little to choose between us. We halved hole after hole (I was partnering Jim), and every time one of us won a hole, I'm darned if the opponents didn't win the next one.

We were all square on the eighteenth tee. 'As it's everything to play on the last hole,' said Jim, as he flexed his arms for the drive, 'what about a bet?'

'Why not?' agreed the D.P.P. man, Webster by name. 'Losers pay for the lunch.'

'I'm on,' I agreed.

We all agreed. Jim drove off. A magnificent effort. Straight as an arrow, something well over two hundred yards.

'Humph!' exclaimed Webster reflectively. He pursed his lips and drove off. A magnificent effort. Straight as an arrow, something well over two hundred yards.

'And if we halve?' asked the Scotland Yard man, Fairlie, as we began to walk the fairway.

Jim had the answer. 'Iain and I will buy brandy for all, you two will buy cigars.'

'Solomon,' congratulated Fairlie. 'If I were not so anxious to have a free meal at your expense, Jim, I think I should be tempted to play for a half.'

That, of course, was my cue, when we reached Jim's ball, two yards behind Webster's, to slice with' my brassie. I swear I did not do so intentionally. Even though the idea of a post-prandial brandy and cigar was attractive I pride myself on being a sportsman in all respects.

Jim yelled an unprintable exclamation. Fairlie and Webster began to shake with laughter.

'I'm beginning to feel hungry, aren't you, Harry?' This from Fairlie.

Webster enthusiastically agreed. 'I'm starting off with smoked salmon.'

'"There's many a slip,"' Jim sourly quoted.

But not where Fairlie was concerned. He took a number two iron and kept the ball dead in the middle of the fairway, twenty yards short of the green, all set for a birdie four.

Another unprintable oath from Jim, but he braced himself up. In spite of a difficult lie he used a spoon to put the ball smack on the green. Unfortunately, it overran the grass and up a steep slope, to trickle into the bunker beyond.

'Followed by pheasant, I think,' Fairlie said reflectively. 'With saddle of mutton to follow.'

'Could choose worse,' Webster agreed in between bouts of ridiculous laughter. He was still laughing as he addressed the ball, but although I prayed (unsportingly, in spite of my previous claim) that he would fluff the easy task of putting the ball on the green, he didn't. It rolled smoothly down the sloping green towards the hole, stopping less than a foot from it.

'Concede,' he airily suggested.

'Like hell,' said Jim. 'Show 'em, Iain.'

Show them! What a hope! A four was in their pocket. I'd have to hole from the bunker to halve. I took out my wedge and went sadly round to the other side of the bunker. What I saw there was enough to make a man weep. The ball was lying in a heel-mark at the foot of a ruddy great Rock of Gibraltar. I'd be lucky to get the damn' thing out, still less put it anywhere near the hole. I hoped the club house didn't charge too much for smoked salmon.

Because the hole was virtually lost already, and whatever I might do could not make much difference, I took a casual swipe at the ball. It sailed up into the air, over the peak of the bunker, and plop on to the green. A moment's agonizing silence, for the bunker obstructed my view, and then a roar from Jim.

'By God!' he yelled. 'A bloody cannon! You've sunk it!'

So I had. My ball had cannoned off theirs, plonk into the hole, for a birdie four.

'You bastard!' sadly exclaimed Fairlie.

Webster replaced their ball, sank it easily for a half.

'I could kiss you,' said Jim. To me, of course.

I can't state as a positive fact that that game of golf was wholly or directly responsible for what happened later, but certainly the sherries, the wine, the excellent meal, and, finally, the brandy and cigars, played an important part in loosening tongues. As we sat round the luncheon table, enjoying the cigars with sensuous enjoyment, Fairlie said:

'Anything new, Newberry?'

'There's a juicy sex murder that's puzzling us.'

'The Franklin girl?'

'Yes. If the line we're following up doesn't lead us anywhere by tomorrow morning I'll be calling on your crowd for help.'

'Always willing to oblige. What's the picture?'

Jim gave an account of the crime which we discussed for the next ten minutes—at least, the other three did. I merely listened. When everything had been said that was to be said, there was a momentary pause. Then Fairlie said:

'As one copper to another, Newberry, we've a problem in the Met. district...'

'Give me a ring if you want any assistance. Always willing to oblige.' A typical Jimsonian remark, this.

'At that I might.'

Fairlie was so obviously sincere the rest of us looked astonished. Conscious of the effort his words had had, he continued: 'You see, one of our own men is involved.'

'Ah!'

'He's been investigating a crime which we're beginning to think he himself committed.'

'It's happened before, and it'll happen again,' Jim pontificated.

The Scotland Yard man nodded. 'Afraid so. What makes this particular case worse is the fact that he's a damn' good man at his job. Given time—a different variety from the one he may get'—the macabre joke was said in a voice that was almost apologetic—'he could achieve a pretty responsible position; at any rate, judging by his work to date.'

'What have you got against him?'

'Not enough, yet. And I'm not sure whether we ever shall. The chief clue is something of his found in a place which we suspect of being connected with the crime. We believe him to be one of a gang. If so, it would explain why there have been so many burglaries in his division during the past two years.'

'You think he's the tip-off man?'

'Yes, giving the gang up-to-date info. on times of police patrols, check points, etc. You know the drill.'

'Too well.'

Fairlie nodded. 'We've submitted the papers to Webster, but the Director agreed that they should be returned for additional evidence. What we have so far won't hold. We've got men from another division tailing him, but so far they've not come across with an additional scrap of evidence. I can't help feeling they don't want to, if they can help it. That's why the commander might not object to having somebody not in the Met. Force. Someone in your C.I.D. for instance. He turned to me. 'You haven't said much, Carter. Don't you agree?'

Jim roared. 'No good your asking him, old boy. He's not a sweeney.'

'Not!' Fairlie rubbed his chin with embarrassment. 'I thought he was on your staff, Newberry.'

'Not him. He's one of the lucky ones, doesn't have to work for a living.' He saw my face. 'Well, not much. He's a writer, a blasted crime writer, at that. You know, Iain Carter. If you haven't read any of his books you ruddy well ought to. They're not much good, but he's a nice bloke.'

'Oh!' Both Fairlie and Webster began to look more and more glum. 'A writer!' He turned to me again. 'You will understand if I ask you to treat anything you've heard today as strictly off the record.'

'Of course,' I assured him.

'You don't have to worry about my old pal Iain, Fairlie. He's almost one of us, by marriage. His brother-in-law is a C.I.D. officer.'

'Indeed.' Fairlie looked relieved. 'What is his name?'

'Detective-Sergeant Meredith, Q division.'

I saw Fairlie and Webster glance quickly at each other, and was suddenly convinced that the man they had been talking about was Edward.

14

By the way Fairlie gulped down the remainder of his brandy I knew that the knowledge of my relationship with Edward was as much a shock to him as the C.I.D.'s suspicions of Edward were to me. I could see him desperately trying to think what to say next.

'Interesting,' he mumbled. 'I don't think I have read any of your books. Of course, I don't get time for much reading. Do you write detective stories?'

'Of a kind.'

'—er—about police detectives or, to use that horrible term, a private eye?'

'Police detectives.'

His short laugh had a hollow ring about it. 'Then it gives you an advantage over your—er—over other writers, to have a C.I.D. man as a brother-in-law.'

'It doesn't, you know. It's hard work to get any information out of him. He usually mutters something about the Official Secrets Act, or whatever it's called. Iain Carter has to rely mostly on books written by ex-Police Commissioners for his dope. Fortunately I usually pin-point the domestic side of police life.'

'Probably the more interesting angle.' Fairlie said this as if he meant it. Perhaps he was right. He went on to amplify. 'Ninety per cent of police detective work is routine. Some of us call it drudgery.' Another short laugh, as he played with his glass. 'Would you be insulted, Carter, if I asked a favour?'

'I shouldn't think so.'

'You might be. Would you please not mention to your brother-in-law what you have just heard? You see, I don't want it to get round in any of the divisions that we are having to keep one of our men under observation.'

'Edward would keep his mouth shut. He's too keen on his work to do anything which might prejudice any part of police work as a whole. But you have my word I'll tell him nothing. Or anyone else, of course.' Probably because I meant this, Fairlie accepted my word. Both he and Webster looked relieved. Jim, too, I thought. It was beginning to dawn on him what a crass idiot he was, from the police point of view, not to have let his brother policemen know in good time that I was not one of their fraternity.

The conversation was expertly steered away from police matters back to golf: i.e. who should partner whom for the afternoon game. After discussion it was decided to have a return match.

This we did. Jim and I won, three and two, possibly because neither Fairlie nor Webster seemed to be as much on their game as they had been earlier on. Nor was I, for that matter, for there was a question constantly in my thoughts which I had to concentrate hard to stop trying to answer there and then. What had Waller found in Reddick's house to convince him that Edward was guilty of murdering Naughton?

As Jim pulled up in front of the house I asked: 'Coming in for a quick one?' I hoped to hell he wouldn't. With Jim it's impossible to have a quick one. It never rests at one, nor is it, or them, quick. One might describe him as a lingerer.

I was lucky. 'Love to, but daren't. The little woman's fixed a date for us both at Chelsea. Old school pal, or something, God help us.'

'Sorry you can't,' I lied. 'Thanks for the game. It's been an enjoyable day.'

He nodded. 'It has been. We'll have another like it, one of these days. S'long, Iain.'

'Remember me to the wife,' I remembered to call after him as he shot off—he always shoots off from a starting position. Perhaps that's why he changes his car every two years. He needs to.

'Hullo, darling.' I might have been away two weeks by the warmth of her kiss. 'Had a nice day?'

'Pretty good. And you?'

She pouted. 'Absolutely ravishing.' She added, inconsequentially: 'Greedy-guts was sick again.'

Greedy-guts was our private name for Robert Iain. 'I don't know where he gets his appetite from.'

'No, darling, nor do I.' She looked at me from under her lashes. 'I suppose you're famished, after a sandwich luncheon.'

'Famished!' I had the grace to look ashamed, and went upstairs to change.

Susan found me in the bath, twenty minutes later.

'What's wrong, darling?' she asked, sitting on the rim.

'Nothing.'

'You're a liar, Iain. Nobody could mistake that far-away expression in your eyes. I saw it as you walked up the path to the front door. Give, or I'll…' She put her hand on the tap which operates the cold water of the overhead shower.

It was obvious that I had to capitulate. 'It's the same old business,' I admitted.

'The Naughton case.' Her eyes filled with alarm. 'But I thought they'd given up the idea of suspecting Lowell.'

'They have, in favour of a new suspect.'

'Who?'

'Edward, unless I'm a Frenchman.'

'Edward!' She compressed her lips. 'This isn't your idea of an after-lunch joke?'

'I wish to God it were.' I gave her an account of what had been said over the luncheon table. I wasn't breaking my word. In common law, husband and wife are one entity.

At first she was indignant. 'How dare they? Edward, of all people! He would sooner die…' The words died away. She began to look frightened. 'They didn't tell you what they found?'

'I think they were getting round to that when Jim told them I was Edward's brother-in-law. As soon as they knew that they shut up like clams.'

'How could anything of Edward's have got into the house?'

'Simple enough. He was in the house, searching it after Reddick's arrest.'

'In that case…' Now she looked puzzled. 'I don't understand. If he was there on official business isn't it possible he dropped whatever it was while searching the house?'

I nodded. 'That thought's been worrying me this past fifteen minutes.'

'Have you any idea whatever what it can be?'

'Not the foggiest.'

'Whatever it is, hasn't the Superintendent the sense to realize how it came to be where it was?'

'It's no good asking me. I can't make sense of anything. Even if finding something should have given Waller the ridiculous notion that Edward may have been the man who broke into Reddicks' house, a glance at Edward's log book should have reassured him that Edward was busy elsewhere.'

'Not after the day's work was over,' Susan pointed out in a pathetic voice. 'First you, and now Edward. Why did that horrible man have to get himself murdered? None of us has harmed him. It isn't fair we should suffer on his account.'

There seemed nothing to say in response, unless to point out that it was typical of this cock-eyed life that more people suffer from other people's faults and foolishnesses than from their own. How many men responsible for creating a war die in the firing-line? No, it's the P.B.I. and theirs which suffer most. Besides, I was not anxious to say more than I had to. I wondered how long it would take Susan to get round to the fact that if I had not broken into the ruddy house the police might never have begun to suspect her brother. I was already feeling guilty enough, as it was.

Even if I was in no mood for talking, she was. If I hadn't known that she had deliberately tried to conceal her mental suffering from me when I was the suspect, I should have felt tempted to wonder if she wasn't more fearful for her brother than she had been for me. Now that she had no reason for hiding her feelings, she didn't try.

All the while I was drying myself and re-dressing she kept up a stream of questions. Was I quite sure nothing had been said about the nature of the object? Wasn't there the least hint? What reason did they think Edward might have for killing Naughton? Was it positive that it was Edward who was suspected?

In between questions she interposed statements. It was certain that Naughton hadn't been blackmailing Edward, if that's what the higher-ups thought. Edward had never done anything anyone could blackmail him about. If Waller and his crew believed that Edward had killed Naughton to avoid paying betting losses, that was too ridiculous for words. The only time he ever backed a horse was on the Derby, and now and again on the Grand National.

'It is too ridiculous,' she continued, with tears in her voice if not in her eyes. 'It doesn't make sense to me that they should suspect him of murder just because something of his was found in that house. Why, if it hadn't been for you breaking in they would never—'

She stopped abruptly. I glanced in the mirror—I was tying my tie—and saw her staring at me. I knew at once that the penny had dropped at last. I was surprised that it had not dropped sooner.

After a few seconds she said quietly: 'I think I'd like a drink, darling. Will you be long?'

'No longer than it takes me to put my coat on,' and I suited the action to the words.

She drew near, and kissed me. I knew the meaning of that. She was apologizing for suggesting, however accidentally, that I was partially if not wholly responsible for Waller's suspicions of Edward.

The kiss also meant that she did not blame me, bless her dear heart. She was much too loyal for that.

To my astonishment Waller 'phoned me the next day.

'May I change my mind about going with you to the C.W.A. "get-together" on Thursday?'

'Of course. Glad to have you. Meet there as previously arranged?'

'I'll be there.'

When I told Susan of this call she looked flabbergasted. 'It doesn't make sense.'

'Not to me.'

Then her eyes began to glow. 'Yes, it does, darling. It means that you were wrong about their suspicions of Edward. It must have been some other man, some other crime, they were talking about. If the Super still wants to go to the C.W.A. meeting it's because...' She stopped. Her lips trembled.

I finished the sentence for her. 'Because he's still suspicious of John Ky. Lowell.'

'Oh, my God!'

She sat down and wept.

Superintendent Waller arrived at 5.40 p.m. I pushed a way through to the bar, Waller following, and ordered a double whisky. Christianna Brand was there, talking with Anthony Gilbert.

'Christianna, I want you to meet Detective-Superintendent Waller of Q division.'

I didn't trouble to speak in a low voice. In sharp contrast with the previous loud buzz of conversation my words were followed by a dramatic hush, then a shuffling of feet as the male members of the Association moved nearer to the guest to meet him and listen eagerly to anything he might presently say on the subject of crime and detection. None doubted that an interrogation would follow as soon as reasonably good manners allowed.

Introductions followed, after which Charles Franklin asked the first question. 'Excuse me butting in, Superintendent, but is it a fact...'

Question followed question. A real, live, acting detective-superintendent was manna for fact-hungry crime writers. I carefully watched Waller's face. At the first sign of his looking irritated or bored I would break it up, carry him off to a quiet corner. Until then he was creating goodwill for himself for when it would be his turn to ask questions.

To my surprise he gave ready if occasionally guarded replies to this bombardment of questions, and did not appear in the least resentful. On the contrary, I thought, he looked pleased, benign. Had he been a cat he would have purred. Once, when he caught my enquiring glance, I'll swear he became embarrassed. A few moments later he introduced a mention of John Ky. Lowell.

'Ah!' he replied, in answer to a question put to him by John Boland. 'Why don't you ask John Ky. Lowell that question? He appears to know all there is to be known of police procedure. Is he a member of the association?'

Having at last brought Lowell into the discussion he asked a few more casual questions, but they were so trivial and careless they would have been a discredit to a newly recruited D.-C. In fact, he puzzled me. He was altogether too casual on the subject of John Ky. Lowell. Either he was a far better actor than I gave him credit for, or his real interest in Lowell was, to say the least, half-hearted.

I gave the members of the association a good run before dragging the superintendent away.

'They would carry on asking questions till the cows come home if you let them.'

'You don't have to apologize for them,' he said condescendingly. 'I respect enthusiasm, and an interest in one's work. If your members are so keen to be factually correct in their books I see no reason for obstructing them, within the limits of security.' He laughed jovially. 'Must not give too many secrets of our profession away. Don't want to give crooks more help than we can. They get too much as it is.'

We talked on commonplace matters for a few minutes. Mechanically, for my part, for I was trying to grapple with the problem of Waller's presence at the C.W.A. According to Edward, Waller had jettisoned the possibility of Lowell's being Naughton's murderer, yet he had taken the trouble to attend the meeting. Why? True, he had asked a few unsubtle questions about Lowell, and had learned less than nothing. There was something about this visit which eluded me.

We went on talking. Unexpectedly, he said: 'Pity your brother-in-law could not have been with us. He would have been amused by so much questioning.'

'He's been through it once,' I pointed out. 'He gave us a lecture on one occasion.'

'Of course. I had forgotten.'

I didn't believe him. He was not the man to forget so easily.

He continued: 'I was talking about hard workers just now, and how much I admire them. Now, he's a hard worker if you like, your brother-in-law. Sometimes, I think he works too hard.'

I nodded, and told myself that it couldn't do Edward any harm to put a good word in for him. 'Yes, Anne—that's his wife—says that golf widows have nothing on her. It's much worse being a detective widow.'

'Time, tide, and detection wait on no man,' he pompously exclaimed. 'Yes, indeed, Detective-Sergeant Meredith subscribes to that maxim. He's a nice house to live in, too,' he added inconsequentially. 'I envy him that. It's nicer than mine. It's a pity he doesn't see more of it.'

This, I happened to know, was a fact. Edward could never have bought the house on his earnings as a detective-sergeant. It belonged to Anne and him jointly, my father having insisted upon giving them as wedding present the equivalent of what he had given Susan and me.

This being essentially a private matter between Anne and Edward I said nothing about it to the superintendent. A momentary silence followed. Waller drained his glass. Reluctantly, I believed. I reached my hand for it.

'The same again?'

'Oh no,' he protested insincerely. 'It's almost time for me to go.'

I glanced in the direction of the windows. Rain was teeming down them.

'In this?'

'Well...'

So I refilled the glasses. As I set them down on the table, he said: 'This is the sort of weather to make one send for travel brochures.' He grimaced. 'Of course, you're lucky, you don't have to wait for the summer to take a holiday. You can go to the Continent whenever you want to, which is fairly often, I hear.'

Something disturbed my consciousness like the clang of an alarm bell. The superintendent was not making conversation for the sake of politeness. Something was moving in that tortuous brain of his, and it spelled danger for someone. For me, I suddenly realized. This seemingly innocuous question about visiting the Continent was not an idle one. Waller was trying to trap me into an admission of some sort or other.

I had a drink, glad now that I had asked for doubles. 'Cheers again,' I toasted, as I tried desperately to think what reply to give. If I said I didn't often go to the Continent it made Edward out to be a liar. If I said I did, this would be to offer to the Super evidence on a plate that I had at least one link with Lowell.

Then it came to me that Edward couldn't have told Waller that I was a frequent visitor to the Continent. He didn't know I was. The cunning devil of a superintendent had laid his trap well.

'Edward is so envious, once a year is frequent where he is concerned. My wife and I have crossed the Channel three times in the past two years, if you call that frequent.'

'It is as far as I'm concerned,' the Super said, somewhat sourly, I thought. 'Doesn't your brother-in-law go, sometimes?'

'He and Anne went over last year, with Susan and me. We did the Châteaux district.'

He looked vaguely at the window. 'Some people are born lucky. When I was a sergeant I reckoned I was lucky to have a week at Brighton or Southend. This year we're going over to Ireland.'

All this was leading somewhere. But where? 'We've been talking about going to Ireland some time or other. Most people I know who have been there rave about it.'

'That's why my missus and I are going.' He sipped his whisky. 'Sergeant going with you again? Or is he still set on the Continent?'

'He hasn't mentioned holidays as yet.'

'Somebody was telling me that the Greek Islands are a paradise. One thing about flying places. You don't have to waste precious days getting there. I must tell the sergeant.'

Greek Islands! Flying! The man was a raving lunatic. As if Edward could afford to fly to Greece for a holiday.

Afford was the operative word! At last I knew the reason for Waller's visit to the C.W.A. meeting. It wasn't me he was interested in; it was Edward. In a round-about way he was trying to pump me on how Edward spent his money—and how much! The missing share in the money stolen from the bank, for instance!

On my way home, nearly an hour later, I appreciated the fact that, had I not known that Waller was regarding Edward as a suspect, I probably should have found nothing significant in the Super's rambling questions about houses and holidays, tastes in drinks, the wisdom of saving up for a rainy day, and so on. For the best part of that time he had kept me answering the most crafty, casual questions, not directly concerning Edward, but which, nevertheless, had somehow managed to be comprehensive enough to include Edward. I was convinced that he had been putting pieces of a jig-saw puzzle together, which would create a faithful picture of Edward to a brain capable of interpreting it.

And Waller's brain was capable. I was no longer in any doubt about that. Remembering his claim that the skilled interrogator can make sense of answers which, to the un-expert, would make nonsense, I began to understand for the first time how and why he had achieved his present position. Evidently I had underestimated him, so I thanked heaven, not only for the fact that he was no longer looking for John Ky. Lowell, but also for that game of golf. Because of my lucky knowledge of Waller's purpose I had been able to slant my answers in Edward's favour.

Nevertheless, I arrived home a worried man.

15

S usan could scarcely wait for me to sit down before questioning
me.

'What did he want?'

'Have a drink—'

She stamped her foot. 'Tell me.'

I could see that she was in a nervy state. 'He's not after Lowell.
At least, I don't think so.'

'Then it's Edward?'

I nodded. 'If he asked me one question about him he asked fifty
or more. In effect, how does he manage to live as he does on what
he makes as a copper? What does he do with his spare time? Etc.,
etc., etc.'

She stared across the room. 'I've done some interrogating, too,
tonight,' she said bleakly. 'Anne dropped in to keep me company.'

'And Edward?'

'Stayed at home, baby-sitting. Said he was too tired to come out,
and there was a programme on the telly he wanted to view.'

'Did he know Waller was with me at the C.W.A.?'

'I don't think he did. Anne said nothing about it, so nor did I.'

I caught myself grimacing. 'What's all this interrogation lark?
What were you trying to find out from Anne?'

She was a long time in speaking. Even then she did not answer
the question. 'Iain, darling, do you think it's possible Edward *did*
kill Naughton?'

'Good God! What a hell of a question!'

'I mean it in all seriousness, dearest.'

'But you can't. Edward, your own brother...' I couldn't finish.

'Somebody killed Naughton, and Edward was out that night. Anne has confirmed that. She particularly remembers that night.'

'Why?' I brutally demanded.

'She told me why she distinctly remembers that particular evening, but the reason is a feminine one, and doesn't concern you. What matters is the fact that Edward didn't return home until after ten o'clock.'

'He was probably out on a job.'

'Naturally, he said he was. But was he? How do we know?'

'Anne believed him?'

'Of course she did. There was no reason why she shouldn't.'

'If Anne can believe him, so can you. I do.'

She could not meet my accusing stare. 'I ought to have faith in him,' she whispered.

'I don't understand you, Susan. It's not like you to lack faith in people. The idea of Edward's killing Naughton is too absurd.'

'He was out most nights preceding the murder.'

'We know he was. On the bank burglary case, trying to trace the fifth man.'

She shook her head. 'Don't you remember? When Edward telephoned on the morning of the murder, to say he was coming over, he mentioned that Waller had called off the search for the fifth man.'

'That's true, he did. But you know what an obstinate devil he is. He was probably convinced there was a fifth man, and was using his own time to try and prove his theory.'

'I wish I could believe that.'

'You must.'

She sighed. 'You men! When loyalties come into a problem you become wilfully blind to normal commonsense reasoning.' She gulped. 'I'm going to try and be like you, and convince myself of his innocence. That would be easy if it weren't for Waller.'

'Waller!'

'Iain, for heaven's sake don't underestimate him, just because you write about undetectives. You may not like him, but he's an extremely efficient detective. Even Edward admits that. If he believes Edward guilty you may be sure he has very good reason to.'

'A few days ago he was just as convinced that Lowell had killed Naughton.'

'I know, but...' She shook her head. 'Now, it's different. Before, he had only Edward's far-fetched theory to work on—and how can you be sure Edward didn't propound it to draw a red herring across his own trail? Now there's a definite clue to Edward's guilt, sufficiently damning to interest Central. Do you think Central would have allowed the papers to go before the D.P.P., or have drawn men from another division to keep Edward under observation, unless the evidence against him had been reasonably strong?'

What she said was true enough, but I was sure that Edward was not guilty of the crime. And it was my fault that he was suspected of it! Oh God! What a thing to have on one's conscience.

'Iain... darling... what is it? You're looking terrible.'

'Susan, it's all my fault...'

In a moment she was standing beside me, her arms about my shoulders, pressing my head against her breast.

'You're not to say that, or think that. Never—never—do you hear me? Besides, if he's guilty—'

'He's not, I'll swear he's not. If I hadn't broken into that bloody house—'

'It was your right to, to protect yourself—' Her voice broke. I felt her trembling, and knew it was time to reverse rôles. She could stand so much...

*

Another semi-sleepless night. I turned and tossed about, developing one hell of a headache in the process. Something had to be done, but what? The same old problem, all over again. As if once in a lifetime wasn't enough.

After some thought I began to see that the circumstances were not the same. There were essential differences between the two problems. In my own case it had been necessary for me only to draw attention away from myself by manufacturing negative evidence that I could not have been the man in Reddick's house. In Edward's case there existed apparent evidence that he *had* been there. It wasn't enough to implicate another, unknown party instead: that would do nothing, presumably, to negative the evidence against Edward. Only the arrest of the real murderer would free Edward from suspicion, perhaps arrest and trial. Thank God, the Director of Public Prosecutions had so far refused to authorize his arrest.

I did not see what could be done. My head grew steadily worse with the effort of concentrated thought. In the end I reached out in the darkness for the tube of Anadins I always keep on my bedside table. Before they took effect my head worsened; I was nearly moved to take two more. I had almost reached the stage of doing so when the hypnotic influence of the tablets worked faster than the analgesic, and I fell asleep.

As so often happens when one does not sleep until the early hours, I woke early; happily without the headache, though. The few hours' sleep having dismally failed to help my subconscious to reach a brilliant solution to Edward's problem, I tackled it once more with my conscious thoughts. All to no purpose. The situation was so completely impossible I didn't even come up with a single suggestion, not even a fantastic one. My brain was just blank. It was like staring into a fog, one of London's own brand of pea-soupers, now fortunately growing rarer. There was damn-all to be seen.

'How is the head?' Susan asked as soon as she opened her eyes.

'What head?'

'You took Anadins during the night.'

'How do you know?'

'I was awake.'

'I didn't know that. You kept almighty still.'

'I didn't want to disturb you. I know what you are if you think you are keeping me awake. You make yourself worse worrying about me.'

'You're worth worrying about. Anyway, the head's gone.'

'And your stupid guilt-complex with it? That is what was keeping you awake, wasn't it?'

I nodded, without indicating which question I was answering.

I don't know! Perhaps I'm a writer by accident, and not born to it. Your born genius seems to be able to work in any conditions; freezing cold, hunger, ill-health, sorrow, any discomfort you can think of. But not me. I need to be feather-bedded to do my best work. Or even to work at all, for that matter. To be coddled, fussed-over, loved, and, above all, to be unworried. Perhaps the answer is, I'm no genius, just a not-too-bad hack.

At any rate, I couldn't work that day for thinking of Edward, and wondering what the hell was to be done. I tried to think what had been found in the Reddick house that was so unmistakably his. A letter addressed to him, for instance? This could easily have fallen out of his pocket and floated under a bed or other piece of furniture, at the time of his searching the house after Reddick's arrest. But this was such an obvious solution that I could not see its being overlooked by Waller, the higher-ups, and Central, and more especially the men in the D.P.P.'s office: barristers trained to regard every piece of evidence through the eyes of counsel for the defence.

I could almost hear one of them arguing with Waller: 'Now, Superintendent, you are on the witness stand. I am counsel for the defence. You have given evidence of finding a letter, under the bed in

Reddick's house, addressed to Detective-Sergeant Edward Meredith. You have told my learned friend for the prosecution that the accused may have dropped this while he was occupying the room during the evenings immediately preceding the death of Alex Naughton. Why are you so sure he didn't drop it at the time he was searching the house after Reddick's arrest?'

'I can't be sure—'

'Wait, Superintendent, wait. Have you looked at the date of the postmark?'

'Yes.'

'Is it dated before or after the time when the accused searched the house?'

'Before.'

'Ah! Now, had it been *after* that date, the envelope might well have been circumstantial evidence that the accused entered the house at some time or other after you had shut the house up, and handed the keys over to Reddick's solicitor. In such circumstances, my client, Detective-Sergeant Meredith, might have found difficulty in giving a reasonable explanation for its presence there. As it is, he has offered a reasonable, a very comprehensible, explanation, which I challenge you to disprove.'

No, it wasn't a letter. I'd stake my life on that. Then was it a button from one of his suits? A shred of material from the same source? His fingerprints? A handkerchief marked with his laundry mark? It could be any one of these things (but most likely wasn't), but, if so, it could not be evidence that he had visited the house after it had been locked up by the police, for the simple reason that he was not the man who had broken into the house, as I well knew. He had not, I was sure, re-entered it at any time after the police had handed over the keys.

But was I sure? I stirred uneasily as the niggling reflection occurred to me that he could have entered it more easily than I. He could have taken an impression of the keys, and had duplicates cut.

I was soon able to dismiss this disloyal conclusion. Why should Edward have re-entered the house? He had no reason to do so. Unless...

Unless he had been doing a spot of private sleuthing. Disgusted with the superintendent's abandonment of the search for that mysterious fifth man concerned in the bank robbery, had he gone back for another, perhaps a more intensive, search? Such a course would have been consistent with his character, that damn' silly notion that a man shouldn't allow himself to suffer defeat.

I shook my head with dismay. If he had done that! You see, I was beginning to admit the possibility.

Two days passed. Nothing happened. Because the normal human being seems incapable of remaining in a state of tension for an extended period of time, the lack of bad news dulled the sharpness of the shock which the discovery of the police suspicions had had upon us. We began to think we had exaggerated the danger Edward was in. When we sat down for breakfast on Sunday morning I noticed that the strained expression had largely vanished from Susan's face. Laughter rose more readily to her lips as she joked with the children.

It being our turn to visit Anne and Edward on Sunday evening, my parents came round to baby-sit. Even if Susan had not earlier reminded me they were coming, I should have known from the behaviour of the children. Goodness knows what went on behind our backs—Susan and I had mutually agreed that it would be more diplomatic not to ask questions—but both Lindy and Robert Iain, we had noticed, always became tremendously excited at the prospect of being looked after by Granny and Grandad. Having imagination, I could make a shrewd guess, especially when I invariably noticed the dust on Grandad's knees, that young Robert Iain was practising to become a jockey. What my father's clients would have thought, could they have seen him, I hesitate to think.

'Remember us to Anne and Edward,' said my father. Robert Iain was already tugging at one arm.

'And kiss Anne for me,' my mother added.

'They are dears,' Susan said, as we got into the car.

It took us no time at all to reach the Meredith home. As we walked up the path to the front door the passing reflection occurred to me that it was not altogether surprising that Waller was envious. It was a nice house; one which suggested a measure of affluence that was not consistent with the salary of a police sergeant.

Edward gave no hint of suffering from a guilty conscience. He welcomed us with more than his usual warmth.

'You're to drive home tonight, Susan,' he told her.

'Why?'

'I'm going to return some of the many drinks I've had at your place lately. No heel-taps tonight, sister.'

'You'll do nothing of the sort,' Susan said with asperity. If there is one thing she cannot abide it is someone who has had one over the eight.

'But tonight's a special occasion. There's one less trouble-maker in the world, so we're going to celebrate. I've a magnum of bubbly for cocktails, and a bottle of Iain's favourite brandy for after the meal.'

Susan stared at her brother. 'Have you come into a fortune or something?' No sooner were the words spoken than she regretted them. I saw that by her expression, and guessed the thought that had produced it. The missing fifth share of the bank robbery?

'Something is probably nearer the mark. A third dividend. With only eight draws yesterday it could mean a hundred or so.'

A hundred or so! Susan relaxed. 'In that case!' she exclaimed.

There can be no surprise about the fact that the next few hours were exceedingly convivial. It was not until I was beginning to think it was time to make a move that I remembered the cryptic remark with which he had greeted us. The talk about a fortune had temporarily driven the matter from my memory.

'By the way, what was that spiel about celebrating the departure of a trouble-maker?' I asked.

'Oh yes! I've been meaning to tell you. Do you remember Ginger Ellison?'

I did. I had used him in one of my Iain Carter books. Of all bad eggs Ginger Ellison was undoubtedly the worst. He was no specialist. There was scarcely a crime in the calendar he hadn't indulged in at one time or another: armed robbery, housebreaking, embezzlement, fraud, attempted rape, the lot. Of his fifty years, he had spent more than half in prison. Edward had twice shopped him.

'He's dead,' Edward continued. 'Last night, about midnight.'

'Somebody do him?' I couldn't believe that Ginger Ellison had died naturally.

'No. He was lucky. A coronary.'

'Where is he now? In the mortuary?'

'No. In his own bed, where he died.'

Anne grimaced. 'Must you talk about such gruesome things? After such a pleasant evening, too.'

Susan laughed. 'Haven't you yet discovered that an evening isn't a real jolly one for Edward unless he drags a corpse into it some time or other? The more unpleasant, the jollier.'

'Where is... was he living? Still in the same house?' What made me ask that question I don't know. A flash of subconscious inspiration, I later decided.

'Yes, and still with the same woman, poor soul. Why she stuck to him, God knows! Damned if she didn't burst into tears when a constable told her the news.'

Susan rose to her feet. 'If they're going to start on their favourite subject of disparaging women, it's time to go.' She caught hold of my ear. 'Come on, woman-hater. Home.'

And I meekly obeyed. That shows how preoccupied I was.

16

I could not forget the death of Ginger Ellison. If only there were some way of proving him to have killed Naughton, neither Edward nor I would have anything more to worry about.

This was no more than one of those casual reflections which come and go like a puff of summer breeze, and at conception it brought a wry smile to my lips. If wishes were horses...

But the damned thought would not be banished. If only...

After all, I argued, Ginger Ellison's reputation was already so bad that a mere matter of murder would scarcely blacken it more. Even if it did, who would be the sufferer? Not the drab he had lived with, a one-time prostitute who was more often drunk than sober. In fact, an accusation of murder might even ennoble him in her opinion, and perhaps make her grateful that he hadn't murdered her first, as he had sometimes threatened, it seemed. He had no known children; his parents were long since dead—of shame, some suggested. If he had other near relatives anywhere, the police had knowledge of only one, a first cousin in Broadmoor.

In next to no time I had persuaded myself that if Ellison could save Edward by accepting the blame for Naughton's murder it might do him a mite of good come Judgment Day—something to put on the credit side, you might say. Certain it was he'd need all the credit there was going, to offset the debits.

All of which was an interesting experiment in the practice of self-deception, but having effectively argued myself into considering the idea of implicating the dead man as something that might help to whitewash his soul, common sense intruded with a pertinent reflection—why the hell was I wasting time in arguing a course which could only be, by the nature of things, theoretical?

I sighed, and sorrowfully agreed with common sense. Even my super-charged imagination was incapable of translating theory into practice. Resolutely, I switched my thoughts away from the fascinating idea.

'Darling,' I began, as we entered the house, 'do you think it might be an idea—'

'No, I don't,' she firmly interrupted. 'You're pleasantly mellow. Just right. Remember tomorrow... You're always so disagreeable the following morning.'

If you think I spent another sleepless night, wondering whether there might, after all, be something in the idea of incriminating Ginger Ellison, you're wrong. As Susan had rightly pointed out, I was pleasantly mellow, and therefore ready for sleep. No sooner had I turned off the lights than I fell asleep. The hour was just before 8 a.m. when I woke up.

'Hey, Susan!' I exclaimed in a frenzy. 'It's nearly eight...'

But, of course, I was wasting breath. Susan wasn't with me, and the tea in the Teasmade teapot was worse than tepid. To judge by the coldness of the sheets in her part of the bed she'd been up at least an hour. That's just one of those things women do: get up at the crack of dawn when there's a family in the house.

I switched on the radio in time to hear the final headline: 'Weather today is expected to remain cold,' when Susan came in. She was carrying a steaming cup of fresh tea, bless her dear heart.

'So you are awake,' she said. 'How tight can a man get at somebody else's expense!' Her kiss robbed the words of malice.

'Tight, my foot! I only had three.'

'Four,' she contradicted.

'Three.'

'Four. I counted them. Pig!' This with another kiss. Unexpectedly, her eyes turned sad. I knew she was thinking of Edward, wondering whether he had killed Naughton.

Something had to be done. I owed it to Edward. Mine was the responsibility for Waller's suspicions of him. It was up to me to prove his innocence; if necessary, by confessing what I had done, and my reasons. This would still mean trouble for him—though the lesser of two evils. Better for him to be carpeted for having too free a tongue than to remain under suspicion of having killed the bookmaker.

After breakfast I sat me down in front of a writing pad and began to write. I'm one of those people who cannot plot out a story unless and until I have a pen in my hand and writing paper in front of me. I think that the mere mechanism of writing reacts on my brain, sets it into motion. As often as not, when I start a new book, I have only the vaguest notion of what I want to write, but as soon as I write the depressing words, Chapter One, my brain begins to tick over.

Old Johnstone was a curious character, says my imagination, and automatically continues: *According to his neighbours he was a miser and never paid a penny for an article if he could get one for a halfpenny—*

But I don't want to start a story this very instant, which I well could. Already, in the few seconds it has taken me to write those thirty words, a vision of old Johnstone has been created in my imagination. I see him with a greasy grey quiff over a receding forehead, an incongruous affectation; grey eyes half hidden by lazy eyelids; a tight mouth; a wispy grey beard that makes the female sex long to get busy with a pair of tweezers...

See what I mean?

I began to write Ginger Ellison's biography, as I imagined it. I wrote nonsense, of course, but that didn't matter: the script was not intended for publication. I ambled on without caring a damn about the gerund, or a split infinitive. Meanwhile, my subconcious was dealing with the problem of finding some way of convincing the police that Ellison, not Edward, nor John Ky. Lowell, had killed Naughton.

I wrote for a full hour without coming up with a glimmering of an idea. Eventually, it was Susan who sparked one off. Accidentally, too. She came into my study with a letter.

'I know you don't mind being interrupted when it's good news. This has just come by second delivery. It's from America.'

I looked at her. 'How do you know it's good news? Have you steamed it open?'

She didn't condescend to answer the accusation. 'Why else should an American publisher write to you? Perhaps he wants one of your books.'

Why, indeed! Perhaps he did. I snatched the envelope from her, and ripped it open.

The letter was from Virginia Publishing Company, Publishers of Good Books.

> *Dear Mr. Carter,*
>
> *Unless you have already made other arrangements, we should be interested in publishing an American edition of your latest novel,* Come If You Dare. *We are prepared to offer you the following terms...*

As if the terms mattered! I threw the letter into the air, jumped to my feet, and seized Susan in a bear-like embrace.

When the excitement was over, and Susan had returned to her chores, I returned to my script. I picked up my pen...

A letter! That was the answer. An anonymous letter to Scotland Yard: Seeing as how Ginger Ellison aren't living no more you might as well know it was him what done in the bookie, Alec Naughton...

It was definitely an idea. I knew from what Edward had told me from time to time that the police never ignore anonymous letters or 'phone calls. Some of them are fakes, or practical jokes, or the work of a man (or a woman) trying to get his (or her) own back on an enemy. But they are invariably followed up, for a worthwhile proportion of the information passed to the Yard by surreptitious means and tip-offs is genuine. Many a criminal has stood in the dock at Old Bailey, or elsewhere, because of vital 'from information received'.

So, an anonymous letter to Scotland Yard to start the ball rolling.

But after that...

Further reflection depressed me. It would not aid my cause if, when the Yard began to investigate the accusation, they found that Ellison's pals could prove a cast-iron alibi for him. Take the false clue I had planted, the Classified Edition. If Ellison had spent that particular Saturday evening boozing at the *Bull and Bush*, or the *Red Lion*, four, eight, a dozen witnesses might testify to the fact.

On the other hand—a glimmer of hope here—suppose the anonymous letter contained information that could be known only to the man who had broken into the Reddick house, and the detective officers who had subsequently investigated the breaking-in. This would be convincing proof that the anonymous letter writer must have been in Ellison's confidence.

I grew more cheerful again. The C.I.D. might choose to disbelieve the alibi of the people at the *Bull and Bush* or the *Red Lion*. Much would depend on the characters of the people concerned. Alibis made by people with records, or of notoriously bad character, are suspect from the start.

The more thought I gave to the idea of the anonymous letter, the more it pleased me, convinced me that it was worth trying. It could do no harm, only good. If it did no more than confuse the investigating team, by creating yet one more line of investigation, that was something in Edward's and my favour.

Unfortunately, on its own, the letter would not be enough completely to free us from suspicion. For that to happen the C.I.D. would need proof beyond question that Ginger Ellison had murdered Naughton. Where was the proof to come from?

I continued to write nonsense as I wrestled with the problem. If I were Waller, I asked myself, what evidence would I need to convince me that Ellison had killed Naughton? Fingerprints would help, of course. If Ellison's fingerprints could be found in the room Naughton was killed in, for instance!

What a hope! The room had been searched for fingerprints at the time of the original investigation. It was extremely unlikely that any prints would have been missed—or if one had been, it was certain that no detective having any pride in his department was likely to admit the possibility. In these circumstances, I had the feeling that the C.I.D. would regard the surprising appearance of a print with justified suspicion.

Besides, even granted that they wouldn't, bar waving a magic wand I didn't see how I was to arrange for the fingerprint of a corpse to be found in the sitting-room of a typical, middle-class suburban home—and this, mark you, after the house had probably been dusted and cleaned a score of more times since the crime. It seemed that I was not only writing nonsense, I was thinking it. But that's the way a fiction-monger's mind works.

'Lunch,' said Susan, poking her head round the door. She had a white smudge beneath her right eye, from which I concluded that she had been making pastry. 'You look as if you've done a good day's work,' she added, staring at the scattered sheets of manuscript.

How wrong can anyone be! I reflected.

*

We usually had tea at 4.45 p.m. 'Do you mind if I leave you for an hour or so tonight?' I asked, passing on my cup for a refill.

'Where are you going?' If there was a tiny furrow of suspicion above her rather lovely eyebrows, its existence was understandable. I'm not one of your men who like sloping off on my own of an evening. I prefer to have Susan with me.

'Here and there.' I didn't care overmuch for that deepening furrow. I added hastily: 'Got an idea I want to work out. The exercise might help.'

'What sort of an idea? Not for a new book. You've always told me that your brain thrives on laziness.'

It was true that I had told her this on occasions. Equally true was the fact that it was the truth. I need to be completely relaxed to do my best thinking. And comfortable. The more comfortable the better.

'It's the exception that proves the rule, my dear,' I explained with bland innocence.

'Not with you, it doesn't, you old stick-in-the-mud.' She passed me back my cup and saucer. 'Are you planning another of your wild schemes to save Edward?'

'Another?'

She was in no mood for levity. 'You know very well what I mean. Are you?'

'Yes.'

'Then don't, darling, please don't. It was bad enough when you risked getting into trouble for your own sake. It isn't right that you should do so for Edward's.'

'Not even though it was my fault he's in the dog-house?'

'I don't care what you say, he may be guilty, Iain, and if so, he... he...' She faltered, and stopped.

I knew what she meant. 'All right. If he's guilty he should suffer the consequences. But I'd take an oath he's not, and if I weren't involved, you'd say the same. You know damn' well you would.'

'I suppose so,' she agreed miserably.

'Look, darling,' I continued, more gently, 'I'm working on an idea that might shift suspicion away from Edward to a third party, and at no risk to me whatever. Don't try to dissuade me, there's a poppet.'

She looked at me with puzzled eyes. 'Do you mean you deliberately intend to involve someone else? But that would be terrible, darling. Wicked.'

I grinned. 'Not when I tell you his name. Remember Ginger Ellison, the chap that's just died? Him.'

'Oh!' The reproach vanished from her eyes. She didn't have any conscience about Ellison, especially if it benefited both her brother and me. 'But can you?' Even a suspicion of eagerness in her voice now. 'Is that possible?'

I shrugged. 'That remains to be seen.'

I was boasting. I didn't think it was possible.

How I came to remember Ginger Ellison's address I don't know. Edward had only mentioned it in passing…'He lived with a woman named Mabel in Penguin Road.'

Perhaps the name of the road remained in my memory because of its unusualness, and its incongruity. I could imagine nothing more unpenguin-like than the sleazy neighbourhood surrounding Penguin Road. Of course, it could be association of ideas which fixed the name in my memory. I have long wished that one of my titles might appear on the Penguin list, but so far I've been unlucky.

Anyway, I made my way to Penguin Road. To avoid drawing attention to myself by asking the way I had first looked up its whereabouts in a London road guide, which I then memorized. Having a bump of locality, and being good at memorizing maps, I hadn't any fear of losing my way.

The road was much as I had imagined it. Narrow, badly lit, depressingly dismal, and smelling of fish-and-chips. The prospect of having to live in it would have been enough to make some people commit suicide. I walked down the length of it, neither too fast nor too slow, and wondered which number had housed the late, unlamented Mr. Ellison.

There was a pub at the far end, *The Ship Ashore*. Seeing that it was only a stone's-throw from the river I thought the name was fair enough. I pushed open the swing doors and entered. The bar was reasonably crowded, but after a quick look nobody took any notice of me. I suspect they took me for a tally-clerk, or a merchant-navy type in mufti. Some of the men I believed to be dockers; others looked like seamen from foreign ships.

'Half 'a bitter,' I told the woman behind the bar.

'Half 'a bitter it is, ducks,' she agreed, and poured one out. It looked so tempting I was glad I had been tempted to step in.

It tasted as good as it looked. I drank half at first gulp. Then I slapped the glass back on the bar, and wondered what the hell I was supposed to do next. Ask which house Mabel lived in?... Edward hadn't mentioned her surname: perhaps she called herself Mrs. Ellison. I could imagine what would probably happen next. Everyone within earshot of the question would stare at me. What the hell does this guy want with 'er? their wary eyes and thoughts would ask. A bloody newspaper reporter, or a saucy sid? Whichever the decision, my presence would have been noted by alert eyes, and docketed in suspicious memories. If any real saucy sids should enter the pub for information, as a consequence of my anonymous letter, it was certain they would be told of the bloke who was asking for Mabel's address a coupla nights ago, and not to sleep wif her neither. But the C.I.D. men wouldn't need to be told that. Who in God's name would want to sleep with her? But the bloke must have had some reason for wanting to find out her address. Guess we'd better make a few enquiries...

I had a second bitter, and wished I could have been sitting down with paper and pen in front of me. What a damned stupid brain for a chap to have, not to work properly without pen and paper. But could I get a glimmering of an idea what to do now that I was where I was? I darn' well couldn't. Even if I should find out Mabel's address without more ado, then what? No more breaking into houses, thank you! Especially in Penguin Road, where I doubt whether anyone could cross the road without someone's noticing it, let alone break into a house. I wasn't even sure if the houses had back yards, or whatever, or how to get into them if there were. Probably only by climbing the fences of all the intervening yards.

Damn and damn and damn, I morosely reflected.

Undeservedly, perhaps, luck was with me. Just as I was on the point of departure a slovenly woman entered the bar, and looked round.

'Anyone going to buy me a drink?' she called out in a whining voice.

The barman scowled. 'If you ain't got the lolly to pay for yourself, 'op it,' he said.

'C'mon somebody,' she pleaded desperately. 'Open yer bleeding pockets for Christ's sake. Just one, to help drown me sorrows.'

'You heard what I told you, I ain't going to have you pestering me customers with your bloody begging. 'Op it, before I chucks you out.'

'Ain't I spent enough in yer bleeding bar, when I had it?'

'Yus, when you had it. Now you ain't, so 'op it.'

'Think of what I spent, and give me one yourself, Bill, just one.'

'It's never just one with you, it's the whole bloody barrel.'

'Just one…'

One of the customers threw a shilling on the counter. 'Give 'er one, Bill, if it'll shut 'er trap.'

'If she starts there'll be no getting rid of 'er before closing time.'

'Well, just for once, Bill. It ain't every night Mabel 'as to sleep with a ruddy corpse…'

So it was Ellison's woman!

17

I must admit there's something to be said for a gadget that not only wakes you up on time but has a pot of tea already for the pouring out. And some silly fossils sigh for the good old days!

I woke up to the alarm bell feeling as fresh as a daisy, thanks to a good night's sleep. I poured out the tea, passed one cup to Susan. She looked a little yawny.

'Didn't you sleep well?'

'I did, once I fell asleep.'

'And that took time?'

She nodded.

'Worrying?'

'A little.'

'Then don't. After tonight I hope—'

'Tonight!' she interrupted. 'What's happening tonight? You're not going out again?'

'I must, sweetheart, but with a little luck it will be for the last time.'

'Promise?'

'Promise.'

She sighed. 'I hope you are right. Is it any use my asking where you are going, and what you propose to do tonight?'

'No more use than it was yesterday. The only difference between yesterday and today, I won't be home as early. Probably about midnight.'

'Midnight!' She bit her lip. 'It seemed as though half the night had passed before you were home yesterday. I couldn't believe it was only nine-thirty.' She sat up with a jerk that nearly upset my tea. 'Let me come with you, as I did when you cased the Reddick house.'

'Not a hope.' And then: 'By God!'

'What is it?'

When I did not answer I felt her fingers dig into my thigh. There was purpose in their tight grip. 'Give me a moment to think, darling,' I pleaded.

'You mean, perhaps—'

'Please!'

She was quiet. For a few moments I gave thought to her suggestion. What she suggested was damningly tempting. Her being with me could make everything more natural, and therefore safer and surer. Just as it had last time. On the other hand, I could not force myself to believe I was justified in exposing her to any sort of risk, however slight.

I had asked too much of her patience. 'You've had ten minutes to think. And for heaven's sake drink your tea before it gets too cold.'

Ten minutes! Unbelievable, but the Teasmade clock confirmed her words. I hastily swallowed the tea; and grimaced. I like my drinks hot and strong or cold and strong, not tepid and/or weak.

This time she punched me. 'Are you going to take me or not?'

Dammit! there was a note of excitement in her voice. 'I'll let you know by luncheon,' I answered with caution.

'No, you won't, you'll let me know now.' She kneeled beside me, her hands tightened warningly.

Sometimes I think there's something of the sadist in Susan. Or perhaps she doesn't appreciate her strength. I saw by her eyes that I was in for trouble.

'Yes,' I quickly yelled.

'Do you mean you'll take me?'

'I'll take you.'

I was just in time. A seraphic smile spread across her face.

'You darling, darling, darling,' she exclaimed as she fell on top of me and wrapped her arms round my neck.

I thought I knew something about women; not much, you understand, but just a little. Especially about Susan. But long before the time came for us to leave the house I had come to the conclusion that I didn't really know the first thing about her.

There was the excited glint in her eyes, the happy lilt in her voice, the quick kisses on my cheek or the back of my neck every time she was near me. Not since the week preceding our honeymoon had I known her to be quite so explosive with anticipatory happiness. All *I* could think of was that I should be ruddy pleased when it was all over, and we were both back home again, relaxed in our respective chairs, with a glass apiece beside us. I had a horrible feeling that I must be beginning to feel my increasing age, all thirty-odd years, in fact. Moreover, I was mad with myself for having been bullied—or wheedled, if you like—into promising to let her accompany me. It wasn't fair to ask any woman to incur the emotional shock which she might have to suffer before the night was through. I wasn't looking forward to it myself.

After luncheon, as soon as she had disposed of the children, she came to the study.

'Iain darling, as a matter of interest, what sort of mischief are we going to be up to tonight?'

By the emphasis she gave to the pronoun you might have thought we were going to a gala performance at the Ballet, or something.

'I'm not going to tell you.'

She looked vaguely surprised. 'Why not?'

'Now that I've been forced to agree to your coming with me, I'd be disappointed if you were to back out.'

'Why should I do that?'

'Because what I hope to do won't be very...' I shrugged. 'Shall I say, pleasant?'

A puzzled expression filled her eyes. 'Do you think that would make me renege?'

'You're a woman, darling. I shouldn't blame you. There are limits.'

Her delighted laughter filled the room. 'You men are the funniest things! Sometimes I wonder what you really think we're made of. But there...' She bent over and kissed me. 'We love you for being so solicitous of our finer feelings.'

The minx! She could scarcely speak for laughing. But abruptly her laughter subsided. 'I want to help save Edward, and you, darling, from heaven knows what trouble. Do you think there's anything in the world could stop me from trying?'

Perhaps she was right. 'I'll give you a hint. To begin with, we're going to an East End waterside pub. I'll give you a pound for every sentence you hear that doesn't contain a swear word.'

'Is that what you are worrying about? Really, darling! After having Edward as a brother!'

I waved an impatient hand. 'And I don't mean a common-or-garden bloody.'

'I'm broad-minded. I've been around. Is that all?'

'No.'

She could see that I did not mean to say more. 'Why did you tell me about the pub? So that I could dress the part?'

I nodded. 'And talk, act, and drink it, darling. No gins-and-French, or anything West-Endy. Just lager or bitter.'

'Why not? You know I like bitter. About clothes. What am I supposed to be?'

'Ex-shop assistant, married to a tally-clerk. Can do?'

She reflected. 'Can do. The blue dress I had last year, with a tuck here and there, and some costume jewellery to give it class. And that Cambridge-blue leather overcoat Father gave me as a birthday present two years ago.'

I grimaced. I never had liked that overcoat. It wasn't Susan. But it was *The Ship Ashore*. I had seen its twin there the night before. 'And that ghastly hat, I suppose. The blue beehive thing.'

'You're lucky I've kept it, after all the insults you've hurled at it. I get the picture, darling. And a smattering of Eliza Doolittle, to round it off?'

'Within reason,' I warned. 'They're not idiots, sweetheart. Far from it. If I know anything they would spot the spurious quicker than we could.'

'When do we start out?'

'About eightish. And now...' I rose. 'I have a spot of shopping to do.'

'Shopping?'

I grinned. 'A wreath, darling. But not for me—I hope!'

The parents arrived promptly at seven-thirty, to babysit. They took one look at us and gasped.

'Where in heaven's name are you off to?' my father asked. 'Fancy-dress party?'

'Something like that,' I agreed.

'But, Susan, dear, you look just like a cloak-room attendant in some awful Soho night-club,' Mother protested.

She couldn't understand why we both laughed.

We said our good-byes and departed. As we sat down in the car Susan giggled.

'What *would* your mother have said if she knew we had a wreath in the boot?'

For once I couldn't match Susan's light-heartedness. Now that we were starting out I knew I was wrong to have her with me; dead wrong, culpably wrong. If anything went awry with my plan, God help us. Policemen weren't two a penny in the vicinity of Penguin Road.

We did not talk much during our journey across London. The fault was more mine than Susan's. Her voice was steady as if nothing out of the ordinary was ahead of us. Mine, on the contrary, sounded shaky; at any rate, to my ears. Besides, I am a born worrier where Susan is concerned, as you've already gathered. Even if nothing happened to us, and I did not see why it should, it was the beastliness, the obscenity, of what I was planning to do that I didn't want her to know about. The mere prospect was making me feel sick.

I parked the car just off the nearest main road to Penguin Road. 'We've about a half-mile to walk,' I told Susan.

'I've got walking shoes on,' she said, and I could almost have believed by the slight catch in her voice that she was laughing at me. 'Is one allowed to take your arm?' she went on. 'Or is that too, too unmistakably U?' She *was* laughing at me.

'Please yourself,' I growled. After all, the damn' business was no joke.

She guessed what I was thinking. 'Don't worry, darling. Just because I'm enjoying myself for the time being, I know what all this means to Edward and you. I'll be serious enough when we get there.'

'Enjoying yourself!'

'Yes,' she confirmed, and now her voice was serious. 'The difference between men and women is man-made, darling. Do you really believe that women are the shrinking violets men are convinced we are? For the sake of our children, and the future of mankind, most of us are content to remain shut up in a domestic vacuum, but if we could follow our inclinations we would share your adventures, fight by your side, do all the things men do, plus. Oh, Iain! If only you could know how happy I am to be with you.'

Perhaps I did know. And because I'm such a contrary cuss, I was more sorry than ever to have her with me. She was too precious to be hurt, mentally or physically.

Each road we went down was more dismal and depressing than the one we had just left. There were more cracked windows, more broken street-lights, more nasty smells, more sleazy people to the square foot, more foul-mouthed children, more mangy, tail-between-the-legs dogs, more distorted radio sets.

'After nearly twenty centuries of Christianity!' Susan bitterly exclaimed, quite out of the blue.

I didn't have to ask her what had produced this enigmatic outburst. I had experienced much the same sort of hopelessness the night before. That anyone should be forced by circumstances to live in such a sordid neighbour-hood! No wonder a small proportion of the people thereabouts didn't care a damn for law and order. The only law they recognized was the law of the jungle. Get it. Never mind how, but get it, and fast. What the hell! Life's short, ain't it? Especially when you have to spend so much of it inside. So get it—and spend it.

'Slowly,' I warned Susan as we turned into Scotland Road.

'Is this the road?'

'No, the second on the right. You can see the fried-fish-and-chip shop on the corner.'

'Why are we slowing down?'

'To find a boy to take the wreath to Mrs. Ellison.'

'Oh no!'

I heard the catch in her breath. 'I warned you, Susan.'

'It's so horrible! Like rubbing salt into a wound.'

'More horrible than having Edward or me arrested?' I asked brutally.

'Of course not!' This was the real Susan speaking, my Susan. 'Do you know the number of the house?'

'No.'

'Then how—'

'That's why I want to find a boy. If he doesn't know the address—but I'll bet you ten shillings he does—he'll ask for it. We'll watch from a distance, and see which house he knocks at.'

Two lads were lounging against the wall of a house ahead of us. 'There are two you could ask,' said Susan.

'Not those two.'

'Why not?'

'We should have to stand under a street light to speak to them. There are some more ahead, where it is darker. Just in case of trouble, we don't want to be identified.'

'You think of everything,' Susan remarked. There was a note of wonder in her voice.

'Be Prepared is my motto. It's the Boy Scout in me.'

We walked on past the two lads. 'Nice bit of skirt,' remarked one. The other gave a wolf-whistle.

Susan pressed my arm in warning. She knows I have a hot temper which blazes out if anyone insults her. I once knocked a man for six who laid a familiar hand on her shoulder one New Year's Eve, just off Piccadilly Circus. Luckily he slunk off, so there was no rumpus.

On this occasion my temper was being held in severe check. Besides which, the lads had expressed admiration, not insults, so why shouldn't they admire my wife? Everyone else did, though more subtly.

We moved on out of the radius of the street lamp, and across the first road on the right. A group of three youths stood ahead, obstructing our passage. They showed no inclination to move. It was too dark properly to see their faces. If we could have I'll swear we should have seen them smirking. It was perhaps fortunate for us I was guarding my temper.

'Anyone want to earn half a dollar?'

'Half a bloody dollar!' One of them spat at the gutter.

'Waffor?' said another, the smallest and youngest.

'Deliver this wreath to Mrs. Ellison in Penguin Road.'

'Her!' A genuine gasp of astonishment from the first speaker. 'What the bloody effing hell d'you want to send a flaming wreath to that stinking old whore for?'

'Not me, chum. I don't know who's sending it. My girl here works in a florist's, so the boss asks her nice-like whether she wouldn't leave the perishing thing for him.'

'Well, why don't you? Ma Ellison lives in the next street, number seventeen.'

I shrugged. 'We was in a hurry, that's why, but okay, if nobody wants half a dollar...'

'Gimme the lolly, I'll do it,' said the young one. 'It'll buy a few fags.'

He stretched out a hand, but the first lad, evidently a leader of sorts, pushed it away. 'Not for half a bleeding dollar you won't. Make it three bob, mister, an' we'll all take it. A bob a nob's our price.'

'All right, three it is. Here's the money. And give Mrs. Ellison this envelope. There's a card inside.'

'Christ!' It was beyond belief that Mrs. Ellison or her man could possibly be worth a card, but three bob was three bob. The leader took the wreath, the envelope, and the money, and the three of them departed on their errand. We followed more slowly.

'Do you think they'll deliver it, Iain?'

'We'll see.'

We reached the corner of Penguin Road just as the lads knocked at the door of number seventeen.

'Come on.' I took Susan's arm and hurried away. 'We're supposed to be in a hurry.'

We walked on, as far as the next turning on the right. We turned into it. From the road-map photographed in my memory I knew we should be able, farther down the street, to turn right again, and, by way of a cross road, reach the other end of Penguin Road.

'Why did you send her a card?' Susan asked presently.

'It isn't the card that matters. It's blank. It's what else is in the envelope that she'll be interested in. Five pound notes.'

'Five pounds! I suppose you have a reason.'

'Naturally. Do you know what my guess is? That she's already on her way to a pub—*The Ship Ashore*, I hope, that being her usual port of call, from what I gathered last night. There she'll remain until closing time—if she hasn't passed out by then.'

'I wish I could understand!' Susan said in a plaintive voice.

'That's where we come in. We're going to take her home, where you're going to put her to bed.'

'And you?'

'That, sweetheart, is my affair.'

My guess was one hundred per cent right. The first person we saw upon entering *The Ship Ashore* was Mrs. Ellison. She was drinking what appeared to be gin-and-water—unless it was a triple gin.

Bill, the barman, gave me a slight nod of recognition.

'What's yours, Gert?' I asked Susan.

'Same as you, Stan.' Susan's quick on the uptake.

We had scarcely raised the glasses to our lips when Mrs. Ellison screeched out: 'Same again, Bill.'

The barman reached for the empty glass and poured out a triple gin. 'Six bob,' he said, holding the glass back from her reaching hand.

'All right, you bleeder, give it me. You know I got the money.'

'I wouldn't have poured it out if you hadn't, so give it over while you still can.'

'Blast you!' The woman drew out from a tattered purse a crumpled ten-shilling note which, I didn't doubt, she had received from the barman less than five minutes back. 'Now give it me.'

'There you are, and take your time over it this time, or we'll be chucking you out afore closing time.'

'Mind your own effing business.'

The barman shrugged and turned away to draw two half pints for another customer.

I noticed Susan looking at me, and saw in her eyes a fuller realization of the unpleasant ordeal I had warned her to expect. In spite of that little shadow she gave me an encouraging smile. I knew I could rely upon her whatever happened.

18

T he next half hour passed much as I had hoped it would. Mabel swallowed her second treble gin, ordered and swallowed a third, which she paid for with silver.

'Gimme another, Bill ducks.'

Bill stared at her. 'Better make it a single. You've only two bob left.'

She leered at him. 'That's all you know, Mr. Clever Dick. What if I tells you I gotta another quid in me purse.'

'All right. Pass it over.' It was obvious from the way he spoke that he did not believe her.

Watched by the rest of the people in the bar, who seemed to share Bill's opinion, she fumbled in her purse. With a quick gesture she slapped another pound note on the bar.

'She has an' all!' exclaimed an amazed voice. 'You struck it lucky, ain't you, Mabel? Don't tell me you've found a bloke to sleep wif.' The sally was greeted with a roar of delighted laughter.

'That's my business.' She raised her voice. 'Hurry up, can't you, Bill. I'm bloody thirsty.'

The frowning barman refilled the glass, passed her change. If she wanted to get rid of her money quickly he was willing as the next man to take it. On the other hand, if his speculative glances in her direction were an indication of his reflections, he was anxious to avoid trouble.

'I think our Bill's trying to decide which is the lesser evil,' I whispered to Susan. 'Turning her out before she gets obstreperous, and depriving himself of what money she has left to spend, or taking what comes.'

'He couldn't be blamed for turning her out.'

How right Susan was. The woman's behaviour grew steadily more objectionable. Not content to keep silent and enjoy her own company, she maintained a shrill one-sided conversation with any man within sight of her wandering, unsteady eyes, and most of her remarks, embellished with the coarsest language, were extremely personal. It said much for the good nature of the majority of the men present that they did not resent her witticisms, but greeted them with tolerant laughter.

Only one customer turned on her. 'Why don't you keep your bloody opinions to yerself and get on with yer drinking?'

It wanted no more than that to transform her into a belligerent virago. 'Don't you tell me to shut up, Mr. Bloody Tim Metcalf. We all knows what you are, you perishing pimp. We all knows why that poor little bastard Amy Simpkins didn't ruddy well return 'ome last year, and what 'appened to her...'

'Shut your bleeding mouth...'

'Hold it, Tim,' snapped Bill. 'Come on, Mabel, you've had enough. Out you go.'

'Aw, let her be,' shouted a man at the other end of the bar. 'You can't blame Mabel for 'aving a drop, Tim. I'd do the same if it was my old woman instead of Ginger what wus stiff.'

Tim Metcalf shrugged. The barman scowled at Mabel. 'All right. You can stop, but one more screech and out you goes, p.b.q., see?'

'Effing lot of bastards, the lot of you!' Mabel shouted. 'Gimme another treble.'

'What about me?' called out the man who had spoken up for her. 'Don't I get nothing?'

A roar of laughter greeted this request. Mabel hesitated, meanness battling with gratitude. 'Give 'im a half,' she said in a sullen voice.

More laughter, and a chorus of shouts. 'What about the rest of us, old girl? Ain't we going to 'ave something for putting up with you?'

But Mabel was deaf to their jocular pleas for a drink, and held out a wavering hand for her seventh treble gin. I began to wonder whether the £5 I had sent to her would be enough to make her drunk. I hadn't known that anyone could drink so much neat gin and still remain upright. I glanced anxiously at the bar clock. The time was nearly ten.

Then suddenly she began to sway to and fro. The barman laughed shortly.

'You've had your lot, Mabel. Get out.'

'Gimme another...' She was speaking with difficulty.

'You heard me. No more. Get out, before I pushes you out.'

'I want... c'mon, ducks, just o—o—one mo—more.'

The barman made a move. I stretched out a hand to nudge Susan, but she anticipated me.

'Does she live near here?' she asked Bill.

'Just up the street. She can stagger that far, or sleep in the gutter for all I care.'

'Is it true her husband has just died?'

'Her hus—' Bill checked himself. 'Yes.'

'Poor woman. No wonder she's drunk more than's good for her.'

The barman scratched his head—to avoid exploding I suspected. Some of the men about us chuckled.

Susan went on: 'Me and Stan'll take her home. What's the number?'

'Seventeen.' Bill shook his head in wonderment that anyone could be so naive.

Susan and I finished our drinks, and moved to Mabel's side. 'Let's help you to your home,' Susan murmured.

The moment we took an arm each she began to rave and struggle.

'I wanna 'nother gin,' she screeched. 'Lemme 'lone, you b——s, lemme go.'

I had underestimated the woman's strength. 'Will you come if Bill gives you another drink?'

Her eyes filled with tears. 'You're pals. I'll come. Just one more large 'un, ducks, a gre' big 'uge double treble,' she mouthed. 'One more, ducks...'

I winked at Bill, who got the message. Keeping his back to Mabel he splashed her glass with gin then filled it with water, and set it down before her. It took her several attempts to pick it up. When she did she swallowed the contents with one loud, disgusting gulp.

'One more...' she began.

I looked at Susan, and nodded towards the door. She nodded back. We took Mabel's arms again, and this time Mabel did not struggle; she was too far gone. On the contrary, her feet began to drag; she was almost a dead weight. I hoped to Heaven that the fresh air would not complete the process of intoxication to the point of complete helplessness.

We dragged her into the street, where we found the pavements wet with a steady drizzle. Nothing could have pleased me more, for it had cleared the streets of all save one man. He was walking away from us, about a hundred yards or so ahead.

As we dragged her along the road towards her home Mabel renewed her struggle; whether to return to the pub or to lie down on the pavement there and then to fall asleep, I could not make out. Fortunately, she had little will left to resist us, and within a few seconds went limp again. Shuddering with disgust I slipped an arm round her waist, and used what strength I had to haul her along, as I would a sack of potatoes. I wished she had been a sack of potatoes. Potatoes, whatever their condition, would have stunk less than she did.

Somehow or other we got her to the door of her house. 'The key!' Susan exclaimed. 'Where's her purse?'

I had seen her pull the purse from her overcoat pocket; but perhaps she had not bothered to lock the door. I tried the handle, and pushed. Thankfully, the door opened. We dragged her into a microscopic hall.

'We'll never get her upstairs,' Susan said with despair.

I had second thoughts about putting her to bed. 'We don't have to. We'll leave her in the kitchen.'

'What about light?'

There was enough light from a street lamp coming through the front door to help us to see what we were doing.

'Leave the door open.'

We dragged her into the kitchen and dropped her in a one-armed Windsor chair. 'I won't be a moment. Keep an eye on things.'

Susan followed me out. 'Iain!' Her voice was sharp. 'Where are you going?'

'Upstairs.'

'Where?'

'To her bedroom.'

'But her husband's corpse—isn't it up there, in one of the rooms?'

'I presume so.' I moved nearer to the stairs.

'No, Iain, oh no! That's too horrible…'

I slipped upstairs before she could say any more.

I joined Susan in the kitchen.

'Let's get out quick.'

'I'm more than ready. This awful place. Look!' The kitchen was worse than the bedroom had been; dirty crockery, dirty saucepans, dirty washing, scraps of food—ugh! It smelled to high heaven of so many vile stinks I couldn't identify any one in particular. Not that I wanted to.

As we approached the front door the light coming in was cut off by a large menacing shadow. We were bathed in a curtain of brightness which made me blink.

'Oh!' gasped Susan.

I gulped.

'What's going on here? What are you doing here in the dark with the door open?'

Keep calm, Iain, I told myself. You've got your answer pat.

'We're on our way out, after bringing her back from the pub, Officer. Just in time. She's completely out,' I explained. 'She's too heavy for us to drag upstairs. We've left her in the kitchen.'

'Don't blame you,' the constable said. 'Do her good. Lucky for her you brought her in. If I'd have found her outside she'd have gone to the cells. I've warned her enough.' He stepped back into the road, switched off his torch, paced on.

Susan caught hold of my hand, squeezed it. We followed the constable out, ostentatiously slammed the door behind us, and walked up the street.

'Talk to me. Tell me what you are going to give me for lunch tomorrow.'

Susan was magnificent. She talked away in a high-pitched, slightly loud voice, using a brittle, pretentious intonation that I swear would have deceived Professor Henry Higgins. We drew level with the slower-moving policeman, then passed him. Susan went on talking. I spent the minutes reflecting. That the policeman, a trained observer, would identify us if it came to the point I didn't doubt. It was not as if he had talked to us in the half dark; he had seen us bathed in the light of his cursed torch. So, of course, had the people at *The Ship Ashore* seen us in a strong light, but it was the policeman I was afraid of, not the others. They might or might not be called upon to identify us, but, if the next stage of my plan came about, it was possible that the constable might report upon having found us in the house.

It was a piece of bad luck his having done so, yet I did not think too much harm had been done. I flattered myself that we had acted as any kindly, neighbourly couple might have done, and if, by chance, a

time check should be made with the barman at the pub, still less would
the police have reason to suspect our motives. We had not been in the
house above five minutes or so. Just time enough, I thought bitterly,
for the bobby to wander round the corner and see the open door.
All the same, had he come round that corner five minutes sooner all
my plans would have been ruined. I shouldn't grumble too much.

We turned a corner, and were soon out of sight of the bobby.
Susan sighed, and spoke once more in her normal, quiet voice.

'Thank heaven that's over! Darling, you were wonderful. There
wasn't the slightest suspicion of hesitation in your voice. I'm sure
he swallowed your story hook, line, and sinker.'

'Why not? It was true, no more and no less.'

'I suppose so.' She laughed, and squeezed my arm. 'I still think it
was fun—except your having to go upstairs. Was it too—horrible?...'

'Let's not talk about it. Tell me, would you go through with it
again?'

She took time to give thought to the question. 'Yes,' she said
firmly. 'If it was for your and Edward's sake.'

What a woman!

Because I was convinced that Mabel was not likely to clean up her
house in the near future, and believing there was no other reason
for haste, I waited another three days before posting an anonymous
letter to Scotland Yard.

The following evening Edward dropped in on his way home.
I was startled to see him, not having expected quite such a quick
reaction. I studied his face, but there was nothing about it to suggest
he had momentous news. On the contrary, he was relaxed and easy,
and never mentioned police matters until at last I grew impatient.

'Anything new on the Naughton case?'

'If so, I've not heard of it. The Super's still wrapped up in it as far
as I can make out, but he's keeping so bloody close-mouthed, I think

he's coming to the conclusion he's chasing a shadow. His temper's so foul everyone's keeping out of his way as much as possible.'

From this I realized that Edward's visit was coincidental, and was not for the purpose of giving me the latest news.

We had a pleasant hour during which I learned that crime in the division was going through one of its few slack periods. I must say, Edward looked all the better for it. He seemed completely to be ignoring the Naughton case. I was not astonished. I knew that he had that enviable faculty of disregarding everything else in the world of crime that did not immediately concern him. Since he had been taken off the Naughton case, to hell with it!

Several days passed. Except for the vague fear that things might not go as I had planned I found life infinitely more pleasant now that it had resumed normalcy, as it were. I came to the conclusion that, in spite of my taste for adventure in literature, at heart I was the peaceful, home-loving type. Unlike the frustrated spinster who writes stories of sexy romance, I was not aware of any feeling of frustration. I was content to leave adventure to lovers of adventure.

Susan, too, was similarly affected. She was cheerful, and infinitely tender. Once again I wondered what I had done to deserve such a woman. I could not remember having done anything in this life entitling me to a very special reward. Perhaps I had been a saint in my immediate past incarnation. It added to my glow of satisfaction to believe this.

Exactly one week after his previous visit Edward dropped in again, later this time. One glance at his face was enough to assure me that he had come with news. But there was something about his expression which worried me. He looked tired and strained, reserved almost. I experienced the nasty feeling that, after all, something had gone wrong with my plans. He couldn't have looked more tense if somebody had tipped him off that he was a suspect. Perhaps somebody had...

I looked quickly at Susan who was with me, the children having gone to bed. I saw by her worried eyes that the same thought had occurred to her. When she kissed him with more than her usual affection I realized that she still half believed him guilty of Naughton's murder and was terribly afraid for him.

'How are Anne and Arnold?' she asked, shakily.

It was proof of his own preoccupation that he was not aware of her anxiety.

'Fine, thanks,' he told her automatically.

'You'll all be coming as usual next Sunday?'

If Edward didn't hear the catch in her voice, and wonder why on earth she should be apparently so apprehensive that he and the family wouldn't be coming, that would be proof indeed, I decided, that something was wrong.

He didn't notice. He nodded absent-mindedly as he filled his pipe. 'Yes, thanks.'

I was conscious of badly wanting a drink. There was something ominous in Edward's tenseness. I thought, too, that his flesh looked grey. He looked like a mentally sick man. Something certainly was damnably wrong.

I poured out the drinks. Meanwhile, none of us spoke a word. The atmosphere was terrible. I glanced at Edward. He was staring at the fire. A nerve in his forehead was pounding away. Funny, I thought with sick inconsequence, I've never noticed it before.

I glanced at Susan. She was looking at Edward. The family likeness was more strongly marked than I had realized. Her face, too, was strained; her pallor unhealthy.

'Cheers,' I said huskily, and drank deeply.

Neither of them cheered me back, but they were quick to lift their glasses and drink deeply. Even Susan, who normally preferred to sip.

'Anything doing?' I asked with simulated casualness that wouldn't have deceived a schoolboy.

He nodded. 'That's what I've come to tell you.' He spoke with forced unconcern. 'The Naughton case is solved. The murderer was Ginger Ellison.'

'You've arrested him?'

An impatient gesture. 'Ellison is dead. I told you about him.'

'So you did. I remember. What's the story? How did you get on his track?'

'An anonymous letter to the Yard. Central rang up Waller, so Waller and Dixon and a man from the local division went to Ellison's house and searched the place. Between the floorboards they found a remnant of a letter with scorched edges. There was enough writing on it to convince Waller that it was a blackmail letter. A handwriting expert compared it with Naughton's handwriting, and is satisfied that it was his. As Ellison's fingerprints were on the letter it's assumed it was sent to him. There you have it. Ellison was probably the fifth man in the bank robbery. Naughton discovered the fact and started to blackmail him, so he decided to rub Naughton out rather than pay him money. The rest you know.'

'And the stolen money?'

'According to investigation he had been spending freely for the past week or so. Most of it went on drink. What was left of it, about twenty-three pounds, was found in a hole in the mattress. The case that had contained the opera-glasses was also found, under the bed.'

'Enough proof for anyone.'

'So the Naughton case is ended?' said Susan joyfully.

'It's officially closed.'

'Let's drink to that.'

'Yes, let's,' he agreed.

All three of us drained our glasses. As we put down our glasses I noticed that the sparkle had returned to Susan's eyes. Even if her brother was guilty he was safe. So was the identity of John Ky. Lowell. Life wasn't so bad, after all.

'Refill the glasses, darling,' she said. 'This is an occasion.'

Of course, Robert Iain had to cry out for 'Mummy'.

'Must be his earache again. I won't be long, Edward. You're not going yet?'

'Not yet.'

Susan went out. We heard her footsteps going up the stairs. I looked at Edward. He was still staring into the fire. What was wrong? I wondered.

'Why did you do it?' he asked.

I looked at him, not knowing what he was talking about. 'Do what?'

'Kill Naughton.'

I chuckled. 'Good, you are feeling better.'

'Better?'

'You looked damnably tense when you arrived. Now that you are joking...'

'It's no use, Iain,' he said bleakly. 'I recognized the opera-glasses when Waller showed them to me this afternoon. Besides, my initials were scratched on the inside of the case that was found in Ellison's bedroom.'

'Good God!' No wonder he had become suspect.

'Unfortunately, I had once lent them to Waller. He recognized them. In consequence, for the past weeks, the Super had believed me guilty, and had been trying to get sufficient evidence against me to arrest and charge me with the crime. It was not until Ginger Ellison was proved guilty that Waller apologized, told me the truth, and asked me how the opera-glasses came into Ginger's possession. I told him they had been stolen from me at the Derby, two years ago. Thank God, he believed me!'

I was too aghast with what I had done to Edward to try to prevaricate further.

'I swear I didn't know they were your glasses, Edward. You don't think I should willingly have tried to implicate you?'

'I couldn't make myself believe you would, but there's no telling what any man will do to save his own damn' life.'

'I tell you I didn't know they were yours. Dammit, man, you're Susan's brother. Isn't that proof enough?'

'Yes, that's right, I am.' He turned over his hands in a gesture of hopelessness. 'I don't begin to understand.'

'Look, Edward, because they were your glasses I'll admit that I was the man who broke into Reddick's house and scattered the place with red herrings. But that doesn't make me a murderer, does it?'

'Then why *did* you break into Reddick's house?'

'Because I...' Then I hesitated. It went against the grain to admit that I was John Ky. Lowell before I had to. 'You'll probably say it's a bloody feeble reason, Edward, but I wanted to see how everything worked out. You know, for the sake of a story; the genuine article, as it were.'

'And the planting of more false clues in Ellison's house? And with Susan's help, too.'

'You know—'

'Of course,' he interrupted impatiently. 'Though I'm the only person that does know—as yet.'

'How do you know?'

A tired, disillusioned smile played for a second on his tight, white lips. 'I happened to call in here for a drink that night. Your parents said you had gone out to some sort of a fancy-dress party, looking like a couple of seedy East-Enders. Since this afternoon I've put two and two together, and if you say I'm wrong I swear I'll spend the next week of spare time proving that the two of you were in that neighbourhood. Well?'

'You wouldn't have much difficulty. A bobby caught us in the house.'

'Bloody hell! And let you get away with it?'

'We told him the truth, that we had helped Mabel home because she was too tight to get home by herself. He believed us.'

He shook his head. 'How did Ellison's fingerprints come to be on that piece of charred letter?'

'I give you two guesses.' I shivered slightly.

'You pressed it against the corpse's fingers?'

'Right, first go.'

'You've got guts, I'll say that for you, Iain. But I think you're a damned swine for dragging Susan into it.'

'I didn't drag her into it. She insisted, and you know Susan. She did it for your sake.'

'For my sake? Come off it...'

'She knew, because I had told her, that Central was tailing you on suspicion. She wanted to prove otherwise.' I raised a quick hand to stop a threatened torrent of questions, and told him briefly of what I had learned at the golf club.

'Then she knows you killed Naughton?'

'Hey! Hold it, Edward. I've told you—'

'It's no use. The piece of letter you left under the floorboards was not forged. It was a real letter, sent on Naughton's notepaper, and in his handwriting. That looks as if you must have torn it from one sent to you, and which you had kept, just in case you might have found it necessary to prove mitigation.' He shrugged. 'There is also this,' he continued, passing me a newspaper clipping.

I had seen it before: the advertisement, for the new Lowell book, from the *Sunday Times*. Wondering why the devil he should reintroduce Lowell into the discussion, I began to feel damnably uneasy. What else had he dug up?

'I've seen this.' I tried to speak casually. 'You showed it to me.'

He nodded, and grinned mirthlessly. 'I haven't forgotten. It was that bloody advert that seemed to confirm my suspicions of Lowell.'

'Well, then?' I cleared my throat, but not successfully. My voice remained husky. 'Just shows how wrong you can be.'

'Does it?' he snapped. 'Look at the other side.'

I did so. On the other side was a half-column of book reviews: Julian Symons' *Criminal Records*. At the tag end of *Best of the Week* was a review of *One Hundred Days Since*.

I grimaced. Symons hadn't been kind to me:

That Iain Carter's *One Hundred Days Since* appears among the *Best of the Week* is fortuitous, due to the recent printers' strike. Only five crime novels were published last week.

That was all, but somebody had underlined in ink the name Iain Carter. Naughton, for sure.

It seemed useless to continue denying the accusation. I shrugged.

A distressed expression settled on his face, as though he had not really managed to persuade himself until that moment that I was guilty.

'What the hell am I to do now?' he muttered. 'Hold my tongue? But how could I remain with the C.I.D.? I should despise myself for the rest of my life.' He passed his hand over his eyes. 'Why was he blackmailing you, Iain? It's hard to think of you having done anything you wouldn't want the police or public to know about.'

'It's not what I had done, but what he had.'

'Him! I don't get you. If it was him—'

'Trouble was, Edward, his name wasn't Alex Naughton.'

'That doesn't surprise me, but what difference does that make?'

'He was really George Poynter, Susan's husband. Legal husband, if you see what I mean. Which makes Susan a bigamist, and our children bastards.'

*

He looked a broken man. 'Give me a drink,' he croaked.

I gave him one; a strong one. I gave myself one, too, but not so strong. It wasn't new to me. I had been through it all before.

Presently: 'Are you sure he was George Poynter? Did he offer you proof?'

'Too much.'

'But he was killed... burned to death...'

'He wasn't. The thief that stole his car was burned, not him. Being fed up with Susan's goodness—he was that sort of a man—to say nothing of the fact that he was up to his neck in debts, and the police were after him, he took advantage of the accident to disappear. Eventually he returned to England. When he settled down here he'd no idea Susan was also back in England until one day he saw her pass his window. That was enough for him. He made enquiries. The next thing that happened—'

'You don't have to tell me. He sent you that letter. Come to the house with the money, or else.' He nodded. 'I'd have done the same as you, every day of the bloody week. God damn him to everlasting hell.' He looked up suddenly. 'Susan doesn't know anything of this?'

'Not a word.'

'Then never tell her, for God's sake. What the eye doesn't see!'

'What about you, Edward? What about your conscience?'

'Make a bigamist of Susan! B———r that! Waller's convinced that Ginger Ellison killed Naughton. Shall we leave it at that?'

'Amen!' I muttered.

After a long pause: 'There's just one thing I still don't understand, Iain. You knew from me there wasn't a breath of suspicion against you. What the hell made you undertake that damn' silly business of breaking into Reddick's house?'

'You were so certain that John Ky. Lowell murdered Naughton I was afraid you'd get around to suspecting me of being Lowell.'

He laughed sombrely. 'All right, I admit I made a boob on Lowell, but I'm not that much a bloody undetective to think you could be Lowell.'

'Why not?'

'You're a good sort, old boy. I like you a lot, and I think you're quite a good writer, but—you don't mind me being frank?'

'Go on.'

'You're not that good a writer. You're no John Ky. Lowell...'

The silly chap went on chuckling. He was obviously beginning to relax.